a

BONE
and a
HANK
of
HAIR

a

BONE

and a

HANK

of

HAIR

LEO BRUCE

ACADEMY

CHICAGO

This edition published in 2019 by Academy Chicago Publishers
An imprint of Chicago Review Press Incorporated
814 North Franklin Street
Chicago, Illinois 60610
ISBN 978-1-64160-271-6

**The Library of Congress has cataloged the previous edition
as follows:**
Bruce, Leo, 1903–1980.
A bone and a hank of hair.

Reprint. Originally published: London: P. Davies, 1961.
I. Title.
PR6005.R673B6   1985   823'.912   85-15837
ISBN 0-89733-176-1
ISBN 0-89733-175-3 (pbk.)

Front cover design: Lindsey Cleworth Schauer
Interior design: Nord Compo

Printed in the United States of America

1

"THERE isn't the smallest doubt," said the tall woman in black, "that my cousin has been murdered."

"And the corpse?"

"Destroyed. Obliterated. Buried. Burnt. Anyhow, beyond discovery."

"Perhaps you know the identity of the murderer?" asked Carolus Deene innocently.

"Of course I do. It was her husband. He has completely disappeared."

"I see. I think it would be best if you told me the whole story."

"I'll tell you what I know. It isn't a lot."

Carolus was inclined to dispute that. To know that someone missing had been murdered and by whom seemed to him a great deal. He did not much like the woman in black. Apart from her downright manner there was something rather ugly in her character which he could not yet define. But he was interested.

"You see, I've been abroad for many years," she continued. "Brazil. My husband is an engineer. Others in the British colony in Rio de Janeiro could afford visits to England every few years. We couldn't. We had three children to bring up. I haven't seen my cousin since the first months of her marriage. So I can't tell you everything that has happened. But I'm sure she's dead.

"She was one of two daughters and her father, Herbert Bright, was devoted to her. He died fifteen years ago and left pretty well everything he had to her, but it was securely tied up. It gave her an income of about twelve hundred a year tax-free, but she could not touch the capital. On her death it would go to her children if she had any; if she left none, it would come to mine. In no case would I have any direct benefit from it. Her father, my uncle, left me nothing at all."

Carolus had heard too much of wills and will-making to be surprised at the suggestion of an old bitterness which had come into his visitor's manner.

"About a year before my uncle's death she met this man Rathbone, and, before I or my husband could do anything to prevent it, he married her."

"Why should you have wished to prevent it?"

"Why? He was after her money. A horrible, long weasel of a man. A clerk of some sort, but from the day they were married he never did another stroke of work. Just lived on her money. Now he has murdered her."

"But, Mrs . . ."

"Chalk is my name."

"But, Mrs Chalk, isn't that rather illogical? If he lived on her money and it died with her, wouldn't he have been defeating his own ends?"

"Not at all. I have said she could not touch the capital. She could not. But there are unscrupulous finance companies who will buy someone's life interest for a fraction of its value—a sort of inverted annuity. I have discovered that two months ago a sum was paid to her by one of these companies by which it became the possessor of her income for the rest of her life. Even if her signature had to be forged during these negotiations it would not be a difficult matter. Anne had round, childish handwriting which anyone could copy. My uncle's solicitors could do nothing about it, so her husband's way was clear. He had what money there was and did what I had always foreseen, killed her. I saw it in his face when I first met him. 'If ever there was a wife-murderer,' I said to my husband, 'it's Brigham Rathbone.' I was right."

"I still don't see how you can be so sure."

"Then I'll tell you. They lived at first in Bolderton, which was then an independent town, not one of the northern suburbs of London. A gloomy little house which had been the lodge of a great estate. I went down to see them there. I cannot tell you, Mr Deene, what a dreadful impression I received. The house was damp. My cousin, who was a small, meagre woman and rather plain, never talked very much, but that afternoon she was positively morose. We wished to discuss family matters, but this man Rathbone would not leave us alone for a moment. I can see him now, sitting in that small stuffy room, which smelt of mildew, and taking in everything."

"What family matters did you wish to discuss?"

"I wondered whether she had heard anything of her sister Charlotte."

"Oh, yes. You said she was one of two daughters. And had she?"

"Nothing, except that Charlotte had been paid the sum of money which her father had left her. You see, she was 'No Good'."

Carolus saw only too well. In such a family "No Good" meant that, if not on the streets, the unfortunate sister was near it.

"It had been a most unpleasant situation for a long time. Charlotte was a year or two older than my cousin Anne, and had first startled her family by disappearing from home for some weeks when she was scarcely seventeen. She was found with a man in Southend. That was the beginning of it. Eventually my uncle forbade her the house; but he left her a thousand pounds

(I think it was), which she probably spent in no time. My cousin Anne wished to have no connection with her, and, so far as I know, she never had. I doubt if Charlotte's alive. I'm told that once a woman takes to that life she has very few years ahead of her. But I was telling you of my visit to Bolderton. I came away full of apprehension."

"Did your cousin write to you after that?"

"Very rarely. She became seriously ill in that damp house. Rathbone wrote and told me that. He was forced to take her to healthier surroundings and they moved to Hastings, where she recovered. I'm a poor letter-writer and we lost touch. In Brazil I had no time for correspondence, and I so disliked Brigham Rathbone that I lost all interest in my cousin. It was not until I was coming home that I wrote to her again. That would be some three months ago. When I arrived, I found that they had moved again, this time to a lonely cottage near the village of Bluefield, a remote place between Canterbury and the coast. As soon as I saw the house I knew why Rathbone had chosen it."

"Why?"

"It was the perfect place for a murder. It was not old; on the contrary I should say it was built shortly before the last war. It was a bungalow of red brick with dark-green paintwork. But it was the site! There was no other dwelling for half a mile and this bungalow, which was called Glose Cottage, was entirely surrounded by great dripping trees. I shuddered as soon as I saw it."

"You had written to say you were coming?"

"Certainly. I had the address from my uncle's solicitor. I wrote and said I should be down on the Thursday afternoon. I did not want to go, but I felt it my duty. I received no reply to my letter and set out on the most difficult journey. It took me several hours to reach Bluefield. You wouldn't suppose such villages remained in England. It was not many miles from the home of Barham who wrote the *Ingoldsby Legends*, and that was what it was like. One of the more horrible of them, I mean, concerned with the supernatural. The people looked like idiots, what there were of them. It was a grey, windy afternoon and the village street was almost deserted. I went to the post office and asked an elderly woman behind the counter the way to Glose Cottage. She stared at me as though I had said something extraordinary.

"'Rathbones, you mean?' she said at last.

"'Yes. That's the name.'

"At first I thought she was not going to tell me. She seemed to be worried by my question. Then she said: 'If you *want* to go, it's nearly a mile away.' I was beginning to lose patience. 'Of course I want to go. I shouldn't have asked if I didn't.' She went on staring at me. 'Nobody has ever asked for them,' she said. 'Is there anything wrong?' I demanded rather sharply. 'Nothing that I know of. You should know all about that.' Then she told me the way. I decided to walk. I doubted if there was a taxi, anyway. I set out on the road the woman had indicated and, except for a farm cart, I never met a soul. It was towards dusk and I found the whole district most unpleasant.

"When I saw the bungalow, I almost turned back. It stood there with trees hanging over it and had a look of abandonment and tragedy. I can put it no more clearly than that. Its red bricks and black shadowy windows and little dark porch repelled me. However, I marched up to the front door and knocked with my umbrella. I stood there knocking and ringing for a long time.

"At last Rathbone opened the door, but only a few inches. I saw at once that he had become an old man. He must have been less than forty when he married Anne just as the war finished. She was then twenty-eight, so the most he could be in years was fifty-five; but he had a grey, unhealthy color like some horrible fungus, and he had lost most of his hair. When I had last seen him, he dressed at least tidily, if in a rather seedy way. Now I could see a collarless shirt, buttoned with a brass stud, and his wrinkled neck, none too clean. He had worn a moustache neatly trimmed when I had seen him; now it had gone, but there was stubble on his chin. He looked at me resentfully and did not open the door any farther. I could see he recognized me, but instead of any greeting he said: 'Annie has left me.'

"'I'm not surprised,' I retorted. 'What a place to bring her to! Where has she gone?'

"'I don't know,' he said, and I almost thought he was going to close the door.

"'Aren't you going to ask me in?' I asked.

"'I'm packing. I've put it all in a sale. She's left me.'

"I pushed right into the house and saw that what he said was true. Everything was in confusion; piles of china were on the table and all the pictures down.

"'Well, this is a nice thing!' I said. 'I've come all this way to see my cousin and find she's not here. Why couldn't you write and tell me?'

"'She's only been gone a few days,' he said. He did not sound particularly sorry . . . or pleased, either. Just toneless.

"'Still, you had time enough. I wrote to you from Brazil and then again a week ago to say I was coming down here to-day.'

"'I thought she would return.'

"We stood there in that half-dismantled room in semi-darkness. I've often thought of it since. I wonder he did not murder me then, as he had his wife. There was no fire and no sign of electricity.

"'Can't we have some light?' I asked.

"He shuffled out of the room and came back with an oil lamp which gave a poor yellow light.

"'Now then,' I said. 'I want to know all about it.'

"'There's nothing to tell. One morning . . .'

"'*Which* morning?'

"'I think it was last Tuesday. She suddenly said at breakfast that she was going to leave me. She gave no explanation. She wouldn't tell me where she was going. She asked if I would drive her to the station.'

"'Oh. You have a car still?'

"'We have always had one. What could I do?'

"'Didn't you try to dissuade her?'

"'No good, with Annie. I know after living with her all these years. Once she made up her mind. I drove her down and she caught the 11.4 to London. I've never seen her since.'

"'Or heard from her?'

"'Not a word.'

"'What had you quarrelled about?'

"'We hadn't quarrelled. We never quarrelled. I don't think she liked this house.'

"'She could have said so, surely?'

"'She did. Often. We were going to move. Then suddenly came this.'

"'I simply don't understand it. I should have thought that Anne was the last person to do anything impulsive. Unless you treated her badly.'

"'Never!' he said with a show of animation. 'I never treated her badly. I was . . . devoted to Annie.'

"I saw no reason to start an argument about that. So I questioned him about where Anne might have gone. He could tell me nothing. So far as he knew, she had received no unexpected letters lately. There was no telephone in the house. He admitted that she could drive the car and sometimes went into Canterbury or Folkestone alone. He could not answer for what she might do there. But he had no reason to suspect anything.

"'I shall inform the police,' I said.

"He didn't turn a hair. 'I've already done so,' he said.

"'What about her sister Charlotte?'

"He shook his head. 'She died five years ago,' he said. 'Annie had lost touch with her. No communication between them for the last four years of Charlotte's life.'

"I didn't know whether to believe him. I was aware of something quite uncanny in the atmosphere. At times I felt that someone was in the hall listening to all we said. It was a beastly house. When I came to realize what had happened, I understood. Somewhere quite near us as we talked, under the soil of the garden perhaps or cemented into the floor, were the remains of the murdered woman. But queer and nasty though I found the atmosphere, I did not suspect that then.

"I spoke to him pretty sharply. 'I'm not leaving England for some weeks,' I said, 'and sha'n't go till I've seen Anne.' He looked at me like a frightened animal.

"After a while I left him. He offered rather grudgingly to drive me to the station, but I refused. I walked back. It was only when I reached the village that I realized I should have to wait nearly two hours for a train. There was another station, Tunney's Halt, only a short distance from Glose Cottage, but Rathbone hadn't mentioned it.

"I am glad of it, now, for during those two hours I heard something which makes the whole thing twenty times more mysterious. I asked if there was anywhere I could get a cup of tea and they showed me a cottage. A nice, youngish woman served me and was far more inclined to talk than the postmistress had been.

"'Oh, yes,' she said, 'I know the Rathbones by sight. I don't think anyone knows them much to speak to. They never come into the village if they can help it. Well, sometimes he pops in with the car to do a bit of shopping, but I've never seen her buy anything here. She always drove away somewhere—Canterbury, I dare say. I've seen her going off many times, but never stopping. They both kept themselves to themselves, but her more than him, from what I could tell. Fred the postman said the same. If he came to the door, he would just say good morning; she would scarcely do even that. I went out there last Poppy Day to collect, and she opened the door and stood looking down on me . . .'"

"I thought she was a little woman?" interrupted Carolus.

"That's what I'm coming to," said Mrs Chalk. "She was a little woman when I went away. This person from the teashop said she was tall. I asked her particularly. 'Quite tall,' she said. Now, Mr Deene, a woman doesn't suddenly start growing; so I thought in a flash what had happened. The woman he was calling his wife in that village was not my poor cousin at all. When you come to go into it all, I shouldn't be surprised if you find there have been others. Look at that case years ago of the man who drowned I don't know how many wives in the bath. Look at Christie. You take my word for it, this one is as bad as any of them. If you had seen his face when I asked where Anne was!"

"I must say that inconsistency about tallness is rather interesting. Did you get any confirmation of it?"

"Well, not really. And, as I'll tell you, there's contradiction to it, too. But this woman was sure. Taller than her husband, she said. However, to go on with my story. I got my train back at last and was thankful to leave that village behind. When I reached London, I decided to go and see my uncle's solicitors and tell them.

"Mr Mumford, the senior partner who had known my uncle, Herbert Bright, was dead. I saw his son, who was somewhat perturbed when I told him that Anne was supposed to have left her husband, but he would not listen to what had been told me about Rathbone's wife being tall. 'People get very confused about these things,' he said. 'I often imagine I have been talking to a tall woman and find later that she is of normal height. It's the shoes they wear and whether they are seen with shorter men. At all events your cousin was with him in in this office a week or two ago.' Then, because I was an interested member of the family, he told me the facts about my cousin's income. She had come with Rathbone to arrange the matter. He had done everything in his power to dissuade them from the step they contemplated, but they would not listen to him. Still, it meant that my cousin was alive some weeks ago. Rathbone must have murdered her after securing the money. Perhaps her body was still in the house when I was there. It's not pleasant to think of it, is it?"

"You say that Rathbone has disappeared?"

"He went the day after my call. Left everything as it was. Did not wait for the auctioneer to fetch his stuff for the saleroom. Just went. His car was found abandoned in London. I have seen the police, but they don't seem to take it very seriously. On the face of it, I suppose it's just another couple disappearing. I'm told that's quite frequent, but I know it's nothing of the sort. If you could have seen that house and the man as I did! 'There's only one thing for it,' I said to the C.I.D. inspector. 'Dig!' I said. 'Dig, my dear man. You'll find her. No doubt of it.' But he said something about tracing them. Tracing! How can you trace a dead woman, I should like to know?"

"It's not impossible," said Carolus.

2

THEIR conversation was interrupted by the entrance with the tea tray of Mrs Stick who for many years had been housekeeper and guardian angel to Carolus Deene. There was nothing angelic in her appearance, however, especially as she eyed the tall woman in black with hostile suspicion. It was her aim, too frequently frustrated, to prevent her employer from involving himself in what she called 'those nasty murder cases', and as Carolus saw the expression on her small dried bespectacled face he knew that she had guessed or overheard enough to see in the visitor a portent of dangers to come.

"What brought you to me?" asked Carolus when his housekeeper had left the room.

"I heard of you from Bonny Gorringer," said Mrs Chalk calmly.

"From *whom?*" exclaimed Carolus, for he had never heard the name.

"Bonny Gorringer. Your headmaster's wife."

Carolus was, it is true, senior history master at the Queen's School, Newminster, and his headmaster had a wife, but he had never heard her referred to by her husband with anything like such familiarity.

"Her name's Ada," he said.

"I know. She's related to my husband. Ada Chalk before she was married. But we've always called her Bonny. Short for Bon Mot, you see. The poor thing believes she's a wit."

"Ah, I see. And she suggested . . ."

"It appears that you have solved a few odd mysteries here and there and Bonny lent me your book *Who Killed William Rufus? And Other Mysteries of History*. She explained that her husband wasn't keen on you involving yourself in the investigation of murder, but as she believes this to be a mere disappearance it would be all right. I haven't yet disillusioned her."

"The school breaks up tomorrow for the Christmas holidays," observed Carolus, "and I have no immediate plans."

"Then get to work," invited Mrs Chalk. "There's certainly one murder here if not more. Personally I shouldn't be surprised if you find a string of them. That so often happens, doesn't it?"

"No. It doesn't," said Carolus sharply. "There have been mass murderers, in the Old World and the New, but no one fortunately can say they happen 'so often'."

"Well, you know what I mean. And in this case I sense it. Rathbone has that stale and squalid quality which one feels Christie and Petiot must have had. He is like some revolting fungus."

"You called him a 'long weasel of a man'."

"Don't pick on my words, Mr Deene. When you find him you will see that there is truth in both of my descriptions. Will you have a go at this thing?"

Carolus considered.

"The only kind of investigation that interests me," he said at last, "is of murder. There is no evidence of murder here. A man and wife realize what money they can on the wife's estate and vanish. They may have a thousand reasons for doing so."

"Rubbish. I smelt murder in that house."

To Mrs Chalk's surprise Carolus took that remark seriously.

"I think I know what you mean," he said.

"And if they've just gone away, why did the wife go first, and where? And why was the woman who supplied teas so positive that Mrs Rathbone was tall, when my cousin was distinctly small? Above all, where are they now?"

Carolus seemed unable to decide.

"It's unusual in some respects," he said, "but it would mean breaking a principle. Let me think it over."

The tall woman rose.

"I understand I shall see you at Bonny's tomorrow night."

Carolus winced at the name and recalled that it was the head-master's custom on the last evening of the Christmas term to invite his staff to enjoy what he described, with well-meaning inaccuracy, as a festive occasion. He had not yet been asked, but he feared the inevitable invitation; Mr Gorringer was scarcely likely to spare one of his usual audience. A large sententious man with immense red ears and an air of self-important amiability, he would certainly be at his most verbose, and Carolus would have to suffer it.

When Mrs Chalk had gone, Carolus sank deep in his chair behind the evening paper while his housekeeper was clearing away the tea-things. But in vain.

"You'll excuse me, sir," said Mrs Stick peremptorily.

Carolus looked up.

"Far be it from me not to know my place," the little woman began. "I'm sure neither Stick nor me wouldn't ever presume to say anything when it was no business of ours. But I couldn't help overhearing a word or two that the person who's just left said. And one of those words was 'murder'."

"Was it? Yes, I do seem to remember. . . ."

"It isn't as though we hadn't put up with it often enough, sir. Police and that coming to the house and you going off and us never knowing whether we'll ever set eyes on you again. I said to Stick just now, I said; if this is going to be another of those nasty cases with corpses and that, we shall have to go, I said. I'm sure I do everything I can to make you comfortable and neither of us can't think why you want to get yourself mixed up in such things. . . ."

"Mrs Stick," said Carolus firmly. "The lady who has just left is a relation by marriage of Mrs Gorringer." His housekeeper stared at Carolus. "She is a Mrs Chalk. The headmaster's wife was a Miss Chalk before her marriage. Does that satisfy you?"

"I'm sure I didn't mean to say anything out of place," said Mrs Stick, daunted by this reference to authority. "Only I didn't know but whether she wasn't one of these murderesses. I mean we've got so that we never know what to think when you have someone come to see you. And as I said to Stick, we don't want any more of that after the last time. Now I've got a nice consum-may for you tonight with a fricassay de poison and a steak grillay. What time would you like your dinner?"

"About eight," said Carolus absently. "Tell me, Mrs Stick, what made you think my visitor had something to do with murder? Did you notice her, I mean?"

"Well, sir, I've got eyes in my head. I must have been wrong, seeing that she's connected with Mrs Gorringer, who's most respectable I'm sure, but there was something *about* that person in black."

"Yes?"

"Something I didn't like. That's what made me speak. She seemed to be *after something*, if you know what I mean. I said to Stick, I said, she hasn't come here for nothing. She had a sort of greedy look, I thought."

"Thank you, Mrs Stick. You're very observant."

On the following evening Carolus prepared, without enthusiasm, to dine with the headmaster, for he had received his invitation that morning. This was an annual event which he would gladly have evaded. Already viewed critically by his colleagues, who resented his large private income, his Bentley Continental car, his too correct and varied clothes and his comfortable home, Carolus forced himself to join in all school activities rather than let it be thought that he felt indifferent or superior to them, but Mr Gorringer's Christmas Party was a trial.

Carolus, a slight pale widower in his forties, an ex-boxing Blue and ex-Commando who sincerely loved his work as senior history master at the Queen's School, Newminster, was always made somewhat uncomfortable by the exuberant pomposity of Mr Gorringer on occasions of festivity, while Mrs Gorringer, with her reputation as a wit, was no less—to be brutal—a pain in the neck. But Christmas, as Mr Gorringer had asseverated in inviting Carolus, comes but once a year, and there was no decent means of escape. Besides, the woman in black would be there.

The evening started innocuously with a cocktail by the drawing-room fire. Carolus wondered how such a watery Martini could reasonably be called dry, but sipped with the rest. Hollingbourne, the maths master, tall with long teeth and a great flat chin, talked in his monotonous bass voice, while his wife looked as though she was worrying about the children, as indeed she was.

Mrs Chalk was the last to enter the room and, when introductions had been made, Mr Gorringer repeated a little joke of his wife's, made when they were first engaged, about the difference between chalk and cheese. It looked like being a jolly evening. Mr Gorringer jokingly carved the turkey and they were served with a wine from some country other than France or Germany, a wine which the headmaster had 'discovered'. What was it? Swiss? Greek? Albanian? Tunisian? Carolus could not remember afterwards, but it tasted of resin and black currants.

"It came to my ears," explained Mr Gorringer proudly, "that certain discriminating bottlers had imported a few barrels only of this excellent vintage and I saw my chance. Deene, my dear chap, I should like the opinion of a connoisseur."

Oh, God! thought Carolus and saved himself with an adjective.

"Very interesting," he said.

Mrs Hollingbourne said "lovely", Tubley, the music master said, "smooth on the palate", and Mrs Chalk said nothing at all.

"So we come to the end of another school year," reflected Mr Gorringer tentatively.

"Yes, indeed," said Hollingbourne.

"We have certainly earned our vacation, I feel. I did my last report today."

"Yes, dear, I heard the explosion," said Mrs Gorringer.

So "the ball of wit was tossed lightly to and fro" until Carolus found himself alone with the headmaster, Tubley, Hollingbourne and a bottle of Port Type from the boundless winefields of Australia.

"I gather," said Mr Gorringer archly to Carolus, "that our friend Mrs Chalk may have found something to intrigue you, my dear Deene?"

"She mentioned some curious circumstances," admitted Carolus.

"Curious, indeed. If one disappearance makes a mystery, what do two disappearances make?"

"A bore, possibly. One can't tell."

Mr Gorringer gave a portentous wink to Hollingbourne and Tubley.

"A bore, Deene? To you, to whom mystery is the very breath of your nostrils? You are surely being facetious. We know you too well, eh, Hollingbourne? You need not feel in this case that you may displease your headmaster by your intervention. This is no squalid story of murder which might bring your name and that of the school into disrepute. There are no corpses here, Deene, such as too often seem to attract your interest. Here is only a mystery, a deep mystery certainly, but not one whose solution calls for dark and undesirable activities on your part. I rejoice that you seem to be interesting yourself."

"What do you know of Mrs Chalk, Headmaster?"

"Mrs Chalk? Oh, she has little or no connection with the affair. She had been out of England for years and only returned a month since."

"Still, what do you know of her?"

"A worthy person, I opine. Not, perhaps, of a social status such as one might expect in the wife of Mrs Gorringer's cousin, Montagu Chalk, but worthy. An excellent mother, I believe."

"Truthful?"

"I should imagine, scrupulously. To be candid, my wife's acquaintance with her has not been profound, but Mrs Gorringer, as you know, has perceptions as keen as her wit and finds nothing to criticize in her cousin's wife except, perhaps, that she seems to have mistaken an invitation to pass with us a day or two for an altogether more expansive proposal. But I cannot see what bearing . . ."

"Oh, none, probably. She told me a very odd story."

The headmaster beamed.

"Then I am sure it is to your taste," he said. "While Hollingbourne and I, not to mention Tubley, take our well-earned relaxation, you, my dear Deene, will be busy unravelling this oddity, this mesh of circumstances which has been brought to you. You will certainly discover the errant pair. You will, I hope, be able to restore them to their friends and family."

"I haven't yet decided to do anything about it."

"But you will, Deene, and I wish you er . . . good hunting, as the expression is, and a happy ending to your pursuit. And now . . . shall we join the ladies?"

They did, and Carolus managed to place himself beside Mrs Hollingbourne. He felt a little tired, and the down-rightness of Mrs Chalk, the sprightliness of Mrs Gorringer—"Bonny", he thought irreverently—would be too much for him. He was wondering in fact whether that name had not been a malicious invention when Mrs Chalk used it, quite loudly, across the room. "Thanks, Bonny," she said for her refilled coffee-cup.

Mrs Gorringer was by no means nonplussed. "*That* old nickname!" she said. "Went out years ago. Puts you terribly out of date. Nobody has used it for a century. My Bonny's gone over the ocean, in fact."

"But the *mots* go on," said Mrs Chalk sharply.

The headmaster introduced a diversion. "I was congratulating Deene," he said, "on having such a nice little mystery brought to his door, an occupation for his Christmas holidays. And one, I am pleased to say, which will embarrass none of us. He has but to discover whither may have fled a middle-aged couple, remote connections by marriage of my wife's."

"The remoter the better, so far as Rathbone's concerned," put in Mrs Chalk with her usual bluntness.

"I told you, Headmaster, that I haven't yet made up my mind whether I can be useful or not."

"By the way," said Mrs Chalk, addressing Carolus across the room, "there is one circumstance I forgot to mention to you yesterday." Her harsh voice and suddenly intense manner held the attention of them all. "When I eventually reached that perfectly awful house of the Rathbones, I knocked in vain for a time. Then I saw an electric bell and rang it persistently. It must have been some minutes before Rathbone at last opened."

"Yes?" said Carolus.

"He did not wish me to enter and I believe I know why. *He had been digging.*"

"What makes you think that?"

"I don't think. I know it. He had hurried in from the garden at the back of the house, and in his perturbed state had forgotten to leave the garden fork outside. It stood in the hall. I could see the muddy water which had run from it. Besides, his boots . . ."

"A horticulturist, perchance?" suggested Mr Gorringer placidly.

"Nonsense! The house was surrounded by wilderness."

"Did he make any reference to what he had been doing?"

"He murmured something about potatoes, I seem to remember."

"Come now, Mrs Chalk," said Gorringer. "You are not going to suggest anything morbid, I trust? You assured us yesterday that all you would ask of Deene was to find your cousin."

"Yes. That's all. Alive or dead."

"Dead?" moaned the headmaster.

"Of course. Dead as a doornail. No question of it."

"I think," said Carolus, quietly, "I think I will see what I can do. Bluefield, you say, beyond Canterbury? Glose Cottage. And the solicitors? Mumble, Gray and Mumford of Booty Street, Bloomsbury? The estate agent who has it in hand? Drubbing of Grimsgate. Thank you. And thank you, Mrs Gorringer, for a delightful evening. Good night, Headmaster. Brighton these holidays?"

"No, no," said Mr Gorringer severely. "At Christmas our own home. I hope . . ."

"Good night," said Carolus, cheerfully grabbing his coat from a vast erection called a hatstand which rose grimly like some hideous ruminant in the entrance hall. "Happy Christmas to you all. Good night."

Before there was more than a rising murmur of response, he was on his way homewards.

3

Carolus set out next day for the town of Grimsgate between Folkestone and Dover, since it was here that Mr Drubbing had his offices. He was a dingy little man who crouched behind a large desk. There was something dry, even dusty, about his skin and colorless hair, something vague in his fish-grey eyes. Carolus explained his identity and calling.

"I see," whispered Mr Drubbing furtively, as though Carolus had come to tell him a shameful secret.

"I want to know about a bungalow at Bluefield called Glose Cottage."

Mr Drubbing did not actually say 'hush', but he looked as though he would like to. His eyes went to the door which was closed.

"What about it?"

"I understand you are going to hold an auction of the effects."

"No. Between you and me that's been cancelled."

Carolus wondered why this information should be between him and Mr Drubbing, but he only asked: "How was that?"

"It's a curious business," said the auctioneer. "I let that cottage to a man called Rathbone."

"How long ago?"

"Between ourselves, it was about three years ago. In 1956. I never liked the place. It was built before the war by a man who wanted to start chicken-farming. He was a sick man when he built it and died there soon after. Even since the war, when every available place has been taken, I haven't been able to sell it. It stood empty for years. Keep it to yourself, but it's in a bad position. Stands quite alone. Then this man Rathbone appeared and rented it. Remained there three years."

"Until?"

"Don't let this go any farther, but one afternoon about six weeks ago he hurried in here and said he had decided to move. Wanted all his stuff put up to auction. You mustn't repeat this, but I could see there was something wrong. The man was nervous. Frightened, I thought at the time. I didn't like it. I tried to put him off. Said it would be weeks before I could arrange an auction. 'My wife's not well and I want to move,' he said."

"Did you know Mrs Rathbone?"

"No. I knew he was married. I've seen her driving their car. But I've never met her. Keep this under your hat, but I wasn't altogether sorry. In spite of the fact that she seemed always smiling, she looked a bit of a gorgon. Glasses. Old-fashioned clothes."

"Tall?"

"Couldn't say. I've only seen her in the car. Anyway, when I told Rathbone it would be some time before I could arrange an auction, he hung about for a bit. Didn't seem able to make up his mind. You mustn't breathe a word of this, but there was something very strange about him. The rent was paid regularly every quarter by cheque, but I always felt there was a mystery there. He seemed to do nothing at all."

"Private income?"

"Must have had. But that's not so usual in these days, is it? And why should they want to live in that gloomy little house miles from anywhere?"

"It is certainly curious."

"Then, just a month ago—I can give you the exact date—he came in here looking as though he'd seen a ghost."

"Perhaps he had."

Mr Drubbing paused and seemed to consider this.

"He certainly looked like it. 'I shan't be able to wait for that auction,' he said. 'I'm leaving at once. Here are the keys.' He handed me one set, though I knew perfectly well there were two. I tried to explain that all this was most irregular, but he seemed quite distraught. I know you won't let it go any farther, but I was worried. I wondered whether I ought to do anything about it. A doctor, police . . . 'What about your furniture?' I said. 'Sell it . . . No, leave it,' he told me. Just to say something while he calmed down, I said I might be able to let the place furnished. He nodded. He hasn't been seen in the district since then."

"What about his wife?"

"She had disappeared some days before. I gather he told people in Bluefield that she had left him."

"And have you let it furnished?"

A twitch that tried to be a smile was on Mr Drubbing's grey features. "Let it furnished? You can't possibly have seen the place. Or the furniture. It has something quite deathly about it."

"I'm thinking of taking it," said Carolus.

"I strongly advise you to think again. Between you and me and the gatepost, it has got a bad name. Perhaps because the man who built it was alone when he died there. Then the disappearance of Mrs Rathbone. How can you account for that? I shouldn't like to stay a night in the place myself."

"It interests me," said Carolus.

"Rather you than me. Of course I can let it to you. In absolute secrecy I must tell you that it still belongs to the family of the man who built it. They've long since given up hope of selling it and are glad to get any price. Then there's Rathbone's furniture."

"Yes. Rathbone's furniture. And effects," said Carolus thoughtfully.

"Say five pounds a week?"

"That will do."

"Hadn't you better see it first?"

"I think not."

"You wouldn't take it if you did. But that's your affair."

Carolus made out a cheque for ten pounds. "I shan't want it for very long," he said.

"Strictly in confidence, I'm sure you won't. Here are the keys. There's no electric light. Main water, yes. Cesspool drainage."

"Thank you. I'll run out there now."

Mr Drubbing leant across his desk. "You're investigating?" he breathed.

"You can call it that."

"The woman's disappearance?"

"And the man's."

"You realize what is being said in the village?"

"I can guess."

"Rathbone was not a pleasant character."

Carolus considered this. Two people, Mrs Chalk and Mr Drubbing, neither of whom he liked, had reiterated their distaste for Rathbone. A "long weasel of a man" one had said; "nervous", "frightened", "something wrong" had observed the other. Mrs Chalk claimed to have seen him at her first meeting as a potential wife-murderer and had talked of Christie, Petiot and Brides-in-the-Bath Smith. Certainly the man had disappeared abruptly but, as Carolus knew only too well, disappearances happened every day from a hundred causes. All the same he would give a great deal to meet Rathbone. He thanked the little estate agent and went out to his car. He had already studied his road map and took the way to Bluefield.

The village itself seemed deserted. Two women hurrying along with baskets were the only beings in sight. The population could scarcely have been more than a few hundred, and at this hour, towards dusk on a December afternoon, the women and children were within doors while the men had not yet come home from work. There was one shop which was also the post office, and the few colored lights in its window for Christmas, instead of making it look festive, gave it a paltry kind of pathos. He saw also a cottage with a signboard announcing that teas were served there. There was an inn, however, firmly closed and without lights now, but at least offering accommodation. Carolus had no intention of sleeping this evening at Glose Cottage before it had been aired and cleaned, so he resolved to return here when he had examined the place.

He entered the post office, as Mrs Chalk had done, to inquire the way. The postmaster, a lugubrious man, stood inappropriately among tinsel festoons, Christmas ornaments and toys. "Yes?" he sighed to Carolus, who asked him brightly how to find Glose Cottage. He stared long and sadly at Carolus.

"It's nearly a mile away," he regretted, as his wife had done to Mrs Chalk.

"I've got a car."

"Oh! I don't know whether you've come to see the Rathbones. If so, I can save you the trouble. They've gone."

"Leave any address?"

"No. They went away very suddenly. Her first. Then him. No one knows where."

"Yes. I have been told the bungalow is empty."

"Was for years before they took it. Well, it's out of the way. Funny their not leaving any address."

"Many letters come for them?"

"No. They scarcely ever had any letters."

"You knew them well, Mr . . ."

"Wallbright. No, I can't say I knew them well. He came in now and again for cigarettes or stamps. I don't remember her ever being in the shop. She was civil enough, though, poor thing. Always had a smile when she drove by."

"Why 'poor thing'?"

"Well . . ." said Mr Wallbright, adequately.

"I've taken the bungalow furnished," announced Carolus.

This startled Mr Wallbright. His chin dropped, making the long face even longer and sadder.

"You're . . . you're going to live there?"

"Stay there, anyhow. Could you tell me the way now?"

"I can tell you the way," admitted the postmaster, but he made no attempt to do so. He was evidently moved by a sort of gloomy curiosity. When he could not suppress this he said: "I can't help wondering why anyone should want to live there."

"Damp?" suggested Carolus.

"It's not the damp. It's . . . You take this road straight on till you come to a fork, where it says to Gray's Farm one way and to Barham the other. Take the left fork as though you were going to Gray's Farm and you'll find it on your left. There's trees round it. It stands quite alone."

"Thank you."

Carolus left Mr Wallbright to stare after him in amazement and started his car. In a few minutes he came to Glose Cottage. It was all that had been said of it. Its bricks, instead of having the cheerfulness of a comparatively new building, were of a peculiarly ugly color, and the dark green of the paintwork was hideous. Dismal cypress trees of the graveyard *macrocarpa* variety thrust their fingers on the very windows and dripped on the neglected garden. The front door was shadowed by a forbidding porch.

The light was fast fading and, not knowing whether he would find a usable lamp in the house, Carolus hurried forward and applied the key. The door opened easily enough, revealing a dark passage-way. It was necessary to strike a match in order to find the door-handles; but, in the first room he entered, a paraffin lamp stood on a large table and there was oil enough in it. Carolus lit the wick and, keeping it low till the glass had warmed, looked about him. This it appeared was the dining-room, for a heavy Victorian table filled most of it; but it seemed to be used as a sitting-room, too, for two misshapen armchairs stood by the empty fireplace, in which there were still dead cinders. The room stank—a stuffy smell like rotting cheese and dead verdure was in the air.

The room on the other side of the front door was no more inviting. Presumably it was called the drawing-room, for it contained a settee and two armchairs covered with damp and colorless chintz, and a quantity of ebonized furniture. Behind it was a double bedroom—brass beds and chamber-pots—while behind the dining-room was a dark kitchen. The bathroom-lavatory was reached by a door in the kitchen, and had apparently been added to the original design, being little more than a lean-to.

This preliminary examination satisfied Carolus. Shivering slightly and thoroughly depressed he turned out the lamp, slammed the front door and made for his car; but in the road he turned and looked back. Certainly there was no sign of any work done by what Mr Gorringer characteristically had called a horticulturist. There was light enough to see long grass growing where once, perhaps, there had been a lawn, and the hedges were untrimmed. A double gate stood before the way to the garage, the doors of which were open, revealing an empty space large enough, Carolus noted, for his car. Behind the house a bare hill rose, but there was no sign of human activity, still less of human habitation. The winter night was coming down on the desolate scene.

Carolus thought again of the bedroom he had seen and wondered whether, after all, he could bring himself to sleep in it. Fresh bedding he would have to buy, for that word 'fungus' which Mrs Chalk had used in connection with Rathbone was all too telling. Perhaps after cleaning and the lighting of fires . . . but there was no doubt about it. Glose Cottage was deathly.

Then, "deathly"? he thought, still standing in the road looking back at the place. What exactly did he mean? Was he tinkering with occultism and suggesting that one could sense in an empty house events, crises, emotions that had once filled it? Was there anything about Glose Cottage that could seriously suggest to a rational mind that a woman had been murdered there? No. Yet, Carolus admitted to himself, he was not without some . . . apprehension, some strong and fearful distaste, at the thought of sleeping there. That stale and chilly air. Those dripping trees. However, he had made up his mind and the thing should be done.

Back in the village he found the cottage with the sign "Teas", entered to find a warm fire and the cheerful, youngish woman whom Mrs Chalk remembered. He ordered tea.

"Would you like some nice hot toast?" said the woman. "I'm afraid there's nothing much else, because we don't get many in, not in winter."

Carolus said he would.

"Just passing through?" asked the woman chattily when she brought his tray.

"No. I've come to stay here."

That caused her to glance at him. Her question had been put without curiosity, but this was evidently a surprise.

"What, in Bluefield?" she said. "I never thought anyone came here if they could help it. Perhaps you've got friends?"

"No. I've rented Glose Cottage."

The woman behaved according to schedule.

"*Rathbones*'?" she asked incredulously.

"They were the last tenants, yes. I've taken it furnished."

Words, Carolus gathered, failed her. At last she found one. "Well!" she said.

"I've just been out to see it. It does seem rather lonely."

"Lonely? It's . . . Did you know them? The Rathbones, I mean?"

"No. I have never met them. Did you?"

"Oh, yes. Well, I used to see her in church on Sundays. Funny old thing she looked."

"Old? I thought she wasn't much over forty."

"She looked a lot older than that. More than fifty, I should have thought. Old-fashioned-looking. Always wore thick glasses and big ear-rings. Never stopped for a chat after the service. She used to sit right at the back, always in the same place, and nip out almost before it was over. He was a bit more sociable. He *has* been known to pop into the Stag. But not her. She never did any shopping in the village, either. People didn't like it. But fancy you going to live in that house! I shouldn't like it, I'm sure."

"No. It's not cheerful."

"It isn't that. You know what they say, don't you?"

What an idiotic yet what a frequent form of speech this was. "No. What?" Carolus gave the prescribed answer.

"They say he did for her, that's what. It was she who had the money, you know. And I mean who's to know, right out there in that place? He could have murdered her and buried her and none the wiser. Then he's off no one knows where."

"It's not very convincing, is it?" said Carolus mildly. "Her remains could so easily be found."

"And you going to live there, not knowing from one moment to the next when you're going to come on something? It's horrible to think of. He may have chopped her up like that case in the papers. Or burnt her bit by bit in the kitchen range. You never know what they think of."

"On the other hand, she may be alive and well."

"She may. Oh, I dare say she may. All I can say is I wouldn't spend a night in that bungalow not for a thousand pounds. Shall I slip out and pop a drop more hot water in the teapot? I'm sorry there's no cake or anything. When are you moving in?"

"Immediately after Christmas. That's if I can get someone to turn the place out in the meantime."

"You'll have a job. There's no one in this village keen on going near it. The only one you might get is Mrs Luggett. She doesn't care what she does as long as she earns enough for a pint or two in the evening."

"Very sensible."

"I don't know about sensible. You never know with her. She might take it on or she mightn't. And if she did, you wouldn't know if she was going to turn up or not. Then again, I don't know what she'd do when she got there. It wouldn't be wise for you to leave any drink about, not if she was there. Mind you, she's a good-natured woman, and all that. She'd help anyone if she'd got it. But when it comes to a job—well, I really couldn't say. You could see her, anyway. She'll be in at the Stag tonight, that's a certainty, because she's got her money today for cleaning out the village hall for the dance on Boxing Night."

"She sounds ideal."

"Oh, I wouldn't say anything against her. If she does have one too many sometimes, there's others do worse, isn't there? And I must say she couldn't do too much for that child of hers after her husband died. He's grown up and in the army now. No, it's only the Name she's got. Well, you know what it is in a small place. But she wouldn't worry about what they say even if there was proof that Rathbone did for his wife. She's not the sort to let that trouble her. She's got a bicycle, too. Yes, you have a talk with Mrs Luggett. She might suit, if you're really going to stay out there."

"Thank you very much. I'll ask her. Tell me, who else knew the Rathbones?"

"Well, no one, really; not to say 'know'. The vicar went there once, I was told, and Rathbone came to the door and was very short with him. They had no calls from tradesmen, but always brought their stuff from somewhere else, by car. Fred Spender, the postman, called once in a blue moon, and I suppose he saw as much of them as anyone. They never had anyone to do any work for them or anything of that. They say the garden's a disgrace. I can't get over you going to live out there, really I can't. It would give me the horrors. Still, we can't all be the same, can we?"

Carolus paid for his tea and, observing that it was six o'clock, decided to seek accommodation at the Stag. He mentioned this to his informative hostess.

"There again I shouldn't like to say," was her judgment. "They're very funny people, Mr and Mrs Lofting. They may be only too pleased, but then again they may not. One thing, if you do stay there tonight, you'll find it clean. I will say that. She's very particular in that way. You could eat your dinner off her kitchen floor. It's a pity they're not more careful in other things. Some that go there, I mean. But there you are. You can't have everything. I hope you get fixed up all right."

Carolus went out into the dark evening air and drove his car into the open space before the Stag.

4

CAROLUS did not find Mr Lofting, the landlord of the Stag, "funny" in any sense that could have been intended by the proprietress of the teashop. He was a heavily moustached man in his thirties who wore a dark-blue, double-breasted blazer with silver buttons and a silver-threaded crest on the pocket which looked as though it meant something. He spoke in a loud and plummy voice and greeted Carolus with man-to-man heartiness. Carolus ordered whisky.

"Isn't that an 'I' Corps tie you're wearing?" he asked when he had passed Carolus his glass.

"Is it? I wouldn't know. I bought it in France," said Carolus truthfully.

Mr Lofting glanced down at his own polychromatic neckwear.

"I'm an Old Babbacombean myself," he admitted.

"Very becoming," said Carolus. "Can you let me have a room for the night?"

"I shall have to ask the wife about that. What did you want? A single room? Just for one night? She'll be down in a minute and I'll ask her. What brings you to this neck of the woods?"

"Curiosity, chiefly."

"Seeing how the other half live? Studying us rustic types?"

"No. I'm curious about one particular matter—the disappearance of the Rathbones."

"Press?"

"No."

"Police?"

"No. Just a nosy parker. Have a drink?"

"Thanks. I will. I could have sworn that was an 'I' Corps tie. You weren't at Rugby, were you?"

"No," said Carolus. "Did you know the Rathbones?"

"The man came in here occasionally. You know, I feel sure I've met you somewhere. Was it in the RHF?"

"The . . ."

"Royal Huntingdonshire Fusiliers. My old mob. Very decent crowd on the whole. I remember just after the war broke out . . ."

Not that, resolved Carolus, and interrupted with such firmness that even Mr Lofting was halted.

"You say Rathbone came in. Did he ever bring his wife?"

"Good lord, no! She was supposed to be a strict T.T. Yes, just after war broke out we were stationed outside Hastings . . ."

"That's the town from which the Rathbones moved here. Did he ever mention it?"

Mr Lofting seemed a little shaken as though he recognized that the opposition was tough, but he was not giving in yet.

"Was it? No. Scarcely spoke when he came in. Secretive type. As I was telling you, we were in this place outside Hastings and there was a fellow in our mess called Glossop, an old Attleborovian, very good scout . . ."

Desperate remedies, decided Carolus. "I've taken the Rathbones' cottage furnished," he announced.

This pulled up Mr Lofting, mess, good scouts and all.

"Taken it?" he gasped. "Going to live there? You must be raving, old man. It's a pest-house."

"Think so? It suits me. I shan't move in till after Christmas, though. That's why I want to put up here tonight, if you can manage it."

"The wife will be down in a minute," said Mr Lofting shakily.

"Good," replied Carolus, and was about to turn away when Mr Lofting made one last rather feeble fling.

"This chap I was telling you about," he said.

"Who? Rathbone? What were you going to say?"

"No. No. Old Glossop. We were . . ."

But just then two customers walked in and, more accustomed to Mr Lofting than was Carolus, they took no chances.

"Pint of bitter," said one, almost threateningly. "What you having, Ted? And a light ale." He turned squarely to Carolus. "Mild weather for Christmas, isn't it?" he asked.

Carolus, moving away from the bar, agreed that it was.

Mrs Lofting joined her husband. Admirably matched, Carolus thought. She was a sleek and *soignée* chain-smoker.

"Yes, we can manage a room," she told Carolus. "We've only been here a few months. Quite an experience, I can tell you. My husband's an aircraft designer really, but we thought we'd try running a country pub. Quite fun, in a way." She touched her back hair. "Bit of a tie, of course. No holidays for us. Still, we keep going."

When Fred Spender the postman came in, and had been identified in an undertone by Mr Lofting, Carolus managed to chat with him over a drink. He was the only person of whom Carolus yet knew—except the woman in the teashop—who had seen Mrs Rathbone from close at hand. He talked willingly enough.

"Yes, I've seen her. Not to say often, but more than anyone else I dare say. She was a big woman . . ."

"That's what I want to know. There are such conflicting reports. You're sure she was tall?"

"Certainly I am. Tall and big-made. Funny-looking old crow. Didn't talk much. Just 'thank you' when I handed her the letters.

But always had a smile. I sometimes wondered whether she drank, she was that cheery-looking. She used a lot of powder on her face."

"Really?"

"Thick, it looked. Grey-haired. Always wore glasses. Big earrings. Drove the car very well. What else can I tell you?"

"When did you see her last?"

"Some weeks ago now. I don't very often have to go out there, and the last time I went it was Rathbone opened the door. He was just the opposite. Gloomy-looking. Seemed half-scared of something; but he would now and again exchange a few words. He told me that morning Mrs Rathbone had gone away. I said I supposed she'd be back for Christmas and he gave me a queer old look. 'I suppose so,' he said and went inside. Personally, I don't believe he's done for her. He didn't seem the type somehow."

Fred was interrupted by the entrance of a very portly woman who bought herself a bottle of stout and sat wheezing heavily on the bench beside them.

"Evening, Mrs Luggett," said Fred.

"Evening, Fred." It was a deep and stertorous greeting. "Been mild, hasn't it?" She had a fine collection of chins and little dark eyes. She looked as though, once seated, she would scarcely be able to rise.

"Come on your bicycle?" asked Fred.

"Of course I did. I can get about."

"She *can* get about," said Fred proudly to Carolus. "You should see her on her old bike."

"Well, why not?" asked Mrs Luggett. "Weight's not everything, my boy. There's some of the skinny ones can't do what I can." She swallowed her stout. "There. That's better," she gasped.

"This gentleman's been inquiring about Rathbones'," said Fred by way of introduction.

"Oh, them!" said Mrs Luggett without interest.

"I've taken their house," explained Carolus. To his delight she was the first person to hear this news who showed no surprise or alarm.

"Oh, you have," she said, and gazed at her empty glass. Carolus refilled all three. He decided to go straight to the point.

"I'm hoping to find someone to clean the place out," he said. Mrs Luggett said "Cheerio", but made no reply to his remark. Her eyes were towards the bar.

"After Christmas, of course," Carolus added.

There was still no response for nearly a minute, then Mrs Luggett wheezed thoughtfully: "How much were you thinking of paying?"

"A pound a day," said Carolus promptly.

"What do you call a day? I've got my own place to do." Still her eyes never left the bottles above the landlord's head.

"Oh, whatever time you can give. I want to move in the day after Boxing Day."

"I'll see what I can do," agreed Mrs Luggett. "I suppose they'd got everything?"

"I'm buying new bedding," said Carolus. "I'm going out there tomorrow morning to see what's wanted. Then the next day's Christmas Eve. I'll be here on Tuesday evening."

"Leave me the keys when you go, then. Better leave them here. I'll go out there and do what I can. They say he did for her, but I don't take any notice of that. More likely she did for him by the look of them. Still, I'll see what I can manage. You want fires lit, and that?"

"Yes, please."

"Well, I dare say I can do that much. I'm surprised the police haven't been round after all the talk there's been; but they may know more than we think. Yes, I don't mind giving the place a dust-over. I should think it wants it after them. Not that I mind what they say . . ."

Anticipating that he might be invited to join the Loftings in a chatty evening meal after closing time, Carolus asked for some bread and cheese in the bar.

"Wish I could remember where I've met you, old man," said Mr Lofting when he was up at the counter. "You're not a member of the RAC, are you?"

"No. Are you?"

"Not actually. But I thought I'd seen you there. Used to go in with a very good type who belonged to it—Old Radcliff-on-Trentian. Must be somewhere else I've seen you. You weren't in Cairo during the war? No? Ah, here's your bread and cheese. I shall think of it in a minute."

Carolus went up to bed before closing time and, rising at eight, was able to pay his bill to Mrs Lofting and escape before further reminiscences were revived. He drove out to Glose Cottage. Even in the gusty daylight it looked as cheerless and bleak as yesterday. Carolus wasted no time and, opening the double gates, turned the big car into the garage and shut the doors. There was no reason to advertise his presence in the house.

Before beginning the minute search he intended to make, he passed slowly through the rooms. The cause of the smell he had noticed—or at least a part of it—was revealed when he opened a door in the kitchen to find a larder with decaying food in it. It seemed that whoever had last eaten a meal in the house had not waited to wash up but had shoved its remains, dirty plates and all, on the larder shelves. Mildew had formed on something that might once have been stew, and a piece of cheese was covered with a substance that resembled lichen. Drawing on gloves, Carolus made a careful examination of this, and saw that stacked on the shelves behind it were a good many tins of various foodstuffs. Yet, what surprised him was that, although all this had been left as though in panic, the bedroom was stripped to the last rag of clothing. One would have thought that something useless would have remained, old worn-out shoes, perhaps, or a battered hat. There was nothing. Not one item of masculine or feminine attire, not a broken suitcase; only the two beds with their bedding neatly arranged and the rest of the furniture.

Carolus examined these beds and, beyond the fact that both mattresses seemed equally dented and worn, he found nothing noteworthy about them. The sheets and pillowcases of one bed were clean; on the other they seemed to have been changed recently, but slept in once or twice, perhaps.

The top of the dressing-table was dusty and a crack in it held a residuum of dust. He scraped this out with a knife and carefully put it into an envelope. He was smiling slightly as he did so. How his more lenient critic would enjoy calling these methods "corny"! But in these rather odd circumstances they were the only methods.

Next he proceeded to another piece of routine work. He searched the outhouse for a receptacle and found an old sack. (He was relieved as he did so to see a useful stock of coal there.) Bringing the sack in, he began very carefully to fill it with all the ashes left in the dining-room fireplace and the kitchen range. It was a long and dirty job, for no cinder was missed, and when he had finished he carried the sack across to the garage and stowed it in the boot of the car.

Then, still wearing gloves, he began a more detailed search, turning out ornamental pots to examine their contents, opening every cupboard and drawer. He found nothing in the dining-room which he preserved, but in the so-called drawing-room was a knee-hole writing-desk with eight drawers in it. He started with the top left one, and running down that side found nothing, not so much as a drawing-pin. It was probable that, if they had been in use, they had been pulled right out and their contents tipped into some receptacle; but, when he reached the bottom drawer on the right, he found it nearly full of papers. There could be only one reasonable explanation. Whoever had emptied the desk had done so thoroughly but, at the last, some distraction or sheer forgetfulness had caused him to omit a drawer.

Carolus did not examine these papers. He would have plenty of time to do so later. But he noticed a chequebook on the top with "Joint A/c" written on it. The cheques were printed "Westlays and Metropolitan Bank, Folkestone". He made a mental note of that.

But he went farther. "Might almost be wearing a deerstalker," he thought, as he pulled from his pocket a magnifying-glass. In none of his investigations had he used such a thing, for it was entirely foreign to his usual methods. He had never believed greatly in forensic chemistry or the use of the microscope or even, except in rare cases, fingerprints; but this was a rare case.

Slowly, methodically, patiently, he began to go over the cloth surfaces of the room, the backs of chairs and the shelves in the bathroom. It took him nearly two hours to satisfy himself, and at the end of that time all he had to show for his work was a few long hairs, which he carefully sealed in another envelope.

He went out to the small garden at the back of the house and found it completely overgrown. Inspection of the area showed no place where the earth had been recently disturbed so far as he could see, though there was a rubbish-heap not far from the back door. This, like the papers in the drawer of the desk, could be turned over at leisure later. He was today chiefly concerned with examining all that might be disturbed by Mrs Luggett if she kept her promise to "give the place a dust" on Boxing Day or the day after.

Finally, he looked in at the garage when he had removed his car, but nothing had been left here, not even an oily rag or an old plug. Carolus locked up the house and returned to the Stag for a drink. He wished to make a telephone call. Mr Lofting was behind the bar, almost in wait for him, it seemed to Carolus.

"Well, old man, been out to your domain? Pretty grim, I should think. You know, I've been trying to remember where on earth we met."

"I shouldn't bother," said Carolus.

"It puzzles me. I have a feeling . . . You a member of the Old Crocks' Club, by any chance? May have been on the London to Brighton run."

"No," said Carolus firmly. Those noisy bores in goggles who were allowed to monopolize a busy road once a year had always seemed tiresome to him.

"I could have sworn you had a De Dion," said Mr Lofting; "but it will come to me in a moment."

"I wonder if I might use the telephone?" asked Carolus.

"Yes, certainly. In our sitting-room. That's the door, on your right."

Shutting the door behind him, Carolus found himself surrounded by group photographs in uniform, in flannels, in shorts, in school caps, in all of which Mr Lofting at different ages figured. Carolus asked for a London number and was answered by a man's voice.

"Gillick? Look here, I've got something urgent for you."

Sloane Gillick, who had recently retired from the fingerprint section of Scotland Yard, was anxious that Carolus should ghost his life-story, *Men I Have Helped to Hang*, for which a Sunday newspaper was offering a fairly large sum. But, though he wanted to conciliate Carolus, he was not pleased to be called on at Christmas-time.

"I'm afraid it has got to be tomorrow," said Carolus. "After Christmas will be too late. Already the only prints we can hope for are in the kitchen, where they may have been left by someone with greasy or oily fingers. All the normal ones on the furniture will have faded days ago."

There was a protesting rattle in the earpiece.

"Come on," said Carolus. "It'll only take you an hour or two. I'll come and pick you up tomorrow morning and you'll be back in town in the afternoon. It's worth twenty quid to me and all expenses."

The rattle grew more indignant.

"Be a good chap," pleaded Carolus. "I'm really interested in this case. The house is going to be cleaned out on Boxing Day and I must have your information before that."

There was something like resignation in the rattle now.

"All right. I'll pick you up before ten tomorrow," promised Carolus, taking advantage of this. "We can talk about your articles on the way down."

Back in the bar, Carolus found Mr Lofting looking triumphant. "I know where it was!" he said. "On television. You were in *Guess My Gag*, weren't you?"

"I'm afraid you'll have to try again," said Carolus. "Now I must run. Got a murderer to catch. See you after Christmas."

He hurried out and drove home to face Mrs Stick.

5

GILLICK kept his promise and Carolus left him at Glose Cottage for a couple of hours with his equipment because, as he said, he liked being alone when he worked. Carolus asked no questions afterwards, knowing that in a few days he would receive a full report. He drove Gillick back to London where, bearing the sack of cinders which Carolus had removed from the fireplace yesterday and the envelope of dust from the dressing-table, Gillick re-entered his Battersea home. "You shall hear before the end of the week," was all he said.

Mrs Stick had been relieved to see Carolus return on the previous evening. "For all we was to know any different," she observed, "you might have forgotten Christmas and everything and gone off somewhere after asking Dr and Mrs Thomas for lunch tomorrow. I've got everything just as it should be. Turkey. Pudding. Old English style."

"Not so very old," said Carolus, "nor so very English for that matter. Before that sentimental Prince Albert started all this

39

turkey-and-Christmas-tree nonsense, it *was* an English feast. Boar's head, Mrs Stick . . ."

"Was it really? Well, I could have done that. Tate de sang liar row T. Anyway, tomorrow it's dindy far see owe marrons, and I think you'll like it."

Carolus dutifully ate some of that uninteresting and coarse-grained bird with his friends Lance and Phoebe Thomas but, like other people without children, found it impossible to make of the meal an "occasion". He was glad when on the Tuesday, as arranged, he could set out after lunch for Bluefield, having told Mrs Stick that he would be in London for a few days.

"Where shall I say, if anyone wants you?" she asked with quick suspiciousness.

"Say you don't know," replied Carolus airily.

"Well, it wouldn't be any more than truth, would it? I was only saying to Stick, we're not to know where you may be flying off to. But we can't none of us help our thoughts, can we?" asked Mrs Stick, darkly.

The weather remained dull and cold, without even the animation of rain or high wind. Carolus saw, as he approached Glose Cottage, that the front windows were open, while by the door was a woman's bicycle. Mrs Luggett greeted him from her knees in the entrance passage, the linoleum of which she was wiping.

"I've done what I can," she wheezed, "but it will never be what I call fresh. There's been fires in every room and the windows open all day, but you can't get the nasty stuffy smell out of the place. You should have seen the larder."

"I did."

"Well, I mean! But it wasn't only that. There's something seems to have got right into it like damp. Your new bedding came this morning and I did the whole bed with disinfectant before I put it on. Were you going to burn the other, because if so, I could do with it after I've sent it to the cleaners. Ta very much. Mind this slippery lino or it'll have you over. I nearly went down myself just now and if I had I don't know how I'd ever have got up again."

Like so many fat people Mrs. Luggett could work hard when she wanted, and the place had been thoroughly scrubbed and polished. Even the pictures had been down, Carolus saw, and the ugly Wilton carpets had had what Mrs Luggett called "a good banging". Yet, as she said, the mustiness persisted. Nothing, it seemed, could free that house of its deathly staleness.

"I've let the fire out in the droring-room because I didn't think you'd want to sit in there; but you've got plenty of coal here." "Here" was the dining-room. "You needn't be afraid of that armchair, because I've banged all the dust out of it."

Panting and gasping, Mrs Luggett paddled out to the kitchen and presently returned to say doubtfully that it was about time she was off. Carolus guessed the reason for her delay.

"Would you like me to pay you by the day?" he asked.

"It would come in handy," said Mrs Luggett, "because I've got some shopping to do."

Carolus had drawn from one of his suitcases a bottle of whisky and some Schweppes. "Have one before you go?" he suggested when he had handed Mrs Luggett her pound note.

"I don't mind," she admitted with a sigh which sounded sorrowful, but was probably ecstatic.

Carolus poured.

"Whoa! Whoa!" cried Mrs Luggett, loudly but not too soon. "You'll have me off my bike going home, then where should we be? Well, cheerio."

"You've certainly cleaned the place up," said Carolus appreciatively.

"I told you I'd do what I could. But it's still not what I should call clean and never will be to my way of thinking. I can't make out this smell that hangs about either. You don't think there's Anything under the floor, do you?"

"I don't know."

"Because that's what I thought it smelt like today. I spoke to him once, you know."

This cryptic afterthought was explicit enough to Carolus, who was accustomed to meeting pronouns unattached and without relatives in conversation of those he questioned. She meant Rathbone.

"How was that?" asked Carolus.

"Well, as it turned out, I happened to hear they'd come from Hastings and I used to know it well. But Rathbone didn't at all like my mentioning it. Spoke to me quite sharp. Then turned round all of a sudden, gave me ten bob and said he didn't want it known he'd lived at Hastings because he'd left some debts there. He was a queer sort. Looked at you as though he was wondering how much you knew."

Carolus nodded encouragingly, but Mrs Luggett's confidences stopped there.

"This won't do," she said. "I must be running along. I've got my chickens to feed. I hope you get on all right. I shouldn't care for it, but there you are." She pulled herself to her feet and made for the door. "I'll be along in the morning," she said, and Carolus heard her heavy breathing till the front door shut behind her.

Left alone, Carolus thought there was something foolhardy about his venture. He could give himself no concise or logical reason for occupying this unpleasant little house. He could not say precisely what he hoped to gain by it; yet he was convinced that it would not be fruitless. He would make a discovery which would throw light on the whole unsavory mystery.

The thing reeked of the abnormal, if not supernatural, which was very foreign to his realistic and practical nature. From the first he had done no more than sense murder; he could find no rational grounds on which to believe in it. Local opinion, Mrs Chalk's conviction, the uncanny nastiness of this house in which the missing couple had lived—none of this was evidence. Yet he was proceeding exactly as though a murder had been committed. He was surprised at himself.

He had wound up the cheap alarm clock on the mantelpiece and could hear its steady metallic ticking as he stared into a bright clear fire. An hour passed before he moved, then he decided to drive down to Folkestone for a meal before turning in.

That night passed uneventfully and the morning brought heavy rain and Mrs Luggett with a bag slung on the handlebars of her bicycle.

"I brought something for your breakfast," she gasped. "You never said anything, but I dare say you can do with it. Seen any ghosts in the night?"

Carolus admitted that he had seen and heard nothing unusual.

"P'raps you will tonight," she said cheerfully.

But two days passed, in which Carolus did little but examine the rubbish-heap in the back garden, turning it over slowly with a fork, but finding nothing to preserve. He went through the papers in the drawer but, except for the cheque book, those told him nothing he did not already know.

On his third night in the house he went to bed early. He slept with a powerful electric torch beside him for no reason except that of convenience. Without electric light in the house he did not wish to fumble with matches and lamp if he had to get up in the night. He slept deeply, but awoke with a start and lay listening. He knew that something unusual had woken him, but for a time he could hear nothing at all. Before getting into bed, he had opened his window a little and drawn back the curtains and was aware of the brilliant moonlight of midwinter in the world outside; but this had a settled look and moreover did not shine upon his bed. Something else had disturbed his sleep. Then he heard the sound of a key being inserted in the lock of the front door. Of course . . . it had been the click of the gate-latch which had broken in on his unconsciousness.

Whoever was about to enter the house was not trying to do so silently. Lying quite still, Carolus guessed the reason. He or she had not supposed for a moment that the house was occupied. Carolus's car was behind the closed door of the garage. There was nothing outside to show that he was here. Was there anything inside? he wondered. He silently moved his arm to see his watch.

Past one . . . with any luck the heat of the long-dead fire would not be perceptible to the intruder.

The door was pushed open and closed. A torch shone in the passage. Absolutely still, yet tensed to spring, Carolus waited. It was all right. The intruder had opened the door of the "drawing-room" and entered. Now Carolus began very slowly and silently to rise from his bed. Thank heaven there were no squeaks in it! He gradually brought himself to his feet and, grasping his torch, began to move on silent naked feet towards the door. It was cold for he wore only pyjamas.

In a few moments he stood at the door of the drawing-room and saw that the light of the intruder's torch was on the one drawer of the writing-desk which contained papers. A hand grasped some of these. Then Carolus switched on his own far more powerful torch. A "long weasel of a man". Carolus had time to see a terrified face and hear an appalling screech, shrill and inhuman, before the man before him dropped to the floor. He had fainted.

Anticlimax, Carolus thought, and yet what more natural? In a house which he had supposed empty with such confidence that he had not even looked around before going about his business, the intruder had suddenly found himself in white light from a torch. Small wonder that the shock had knocked him out. Carolus went quietly to work. He hurriedly searched the inert body but found no arms. He then brought in the paraffin lamp and lit it. Finally he carried a jug of water from the kitchen and threw it lightly in the man's face. Rathbone gasped. As consciousness returned to him he stared at Carolus from the floor, still in abject terror.

"Better sit," said Carolus, and helped the man to a chair. Then he brought in the whisky bottle which stood on the dining-room table and poured out a peg. "Take it slowly," he warned.

It struck Carolus afterwards as ironic that the first words that Rathbone spoke to him were: "Thank you."

"Come for your cheque book, I suppose," said Carolus chattily, as he took a seat between Rathbone and the door. "You could scarcely write for a new one, could you?"

Rathbone did not answer.

"Where's your wife?" asked Carolus as casually as he could.

"I . . . haven't seen her."

"I needn't ask where you have been or where you're going. The police will find you in a couple of days when they need to. But I would like to know why you rushed away from here."

"Who are you?"

"My name's Deene. I've taken your house furnished. I'm interested in you, Mr Rathbone. There are a lot of things I want to ask you. How, for instance, your wife managed suddenly to grow so much taller after she came to live here? She was a small woman when you married her."

Rathbone stared as though he were in the mesmeric gaze of a snake. He did not speak. Perhaps, Carolus thought, he was unable to. He looked as though he might faint again.

"Why, too, do you come here at what can fairly be called the 'dead of night' to look for your cheque book?"

"I forgot it, when I left."

"I believe you. You overlooked the last drawer. But what was to prevent you coming openly to pick it up? What are you concealing, Mr Rathbone?"

Carolus examined the narrow, weak face. Yes, this man could have murdered a woman. Mrs Chalk had exaggerated, but there was a timid cunning, a cowardly greed in those eyes.

"This place is going to be pulled apart when it is searched," said Carolus. "Every inch of the garden. Every scrap of concrete. Every floorboard."

Still that transfixed stare which could mean everything or nothing. The interview began to seem futile. It was scarcely likely, whatever the circumstances, that Rathbone would answer the questions put to him, and a man so obviously frightened all the time would not give himself away on any particular point. But presently he spoke. "Do you think I murdered my wife?" he asked.

"I don't know. I don't even know that she's dead. But I know you're concealing a great deal. And I know you're very, very frightened, Mr Rathbone."

"I didn't know there was anyone here," he explained with sad resignation.

"It's not that. I startled you but your fear goes far deeper than that. What are you afraid of?"

When Rathbone spoke it was in a strange faraway tone as though he was recalling something from the past.

"I was very fond of her," he said, and Carolus remembered that Mrs Chalk had reported the same words. "You . . . no one should think I murdered her."

"Is she alive then?"

Rathbone seemed to pull himself together.

"I haven't seen her," he said.

"Since?"

"Since she left me. Weeks ago."

"Why did you cancel the auction of your furniture?"

"I thought . . . I hoped she might come back."

"You didn't tell Mrs Chalk that."

"You know Mrs Chalk, then." It was not a question but a wistful realization of something unpleasant—another blow of fate.

"She is convinced that you have murdered her cousin."

Rathbone, looking downwards, made a curious reply. "She never liked me," he said in a regretful voice.

Carolus, shivering in the damp night air, went to the entrance passage and pulled his overcoat from a hook. When he returned, he saw that Rathbone had his head in his hands in an attitude of despair.

"Who are you? Why do you ask me questions?" Rathbone said, suddenly looking up.

"Because I am going to find out the truth. The whole truth, Mr Rathbone. About the woman you married and about the woman with whom you lived here. I don't know yet about Hastings, but I shall. Were you there with the first or the second? Or with someone different altogether? I shall know in time. I shall also know where to look for this woman, or these two or three women . . . if they are alive!"

A cunning look, almost a leer, came unexpectedly to Rathbone's face. "You're very sure of yourself," he said.

"I'm very determined."

"Why?"

It was a devastating question and Carolus knew it. "Because I've made it my business to find out," he answered rather feebly.

"I wish you joy of that," said Rathbone lugubriously.

The clock on the dining-room mantelpiece was audible as the two men sat without speaking. Then Rathbone did an unexpected thing. He stood up and said, "I'm going now." There was a finality in the words which startled Carolus. This man could be resolute, too, when he chose.

There was nothing to be done about it. Hold him by force? Follow him? Get in touch with the police? All impossible and rather absurd. Carolus did not even know whether the police were looking for Rathbone, and it was a mile to a public telephone in the village square at Bluefield. He had no right to interfere with the other's movements and, indeed, no desire to do so. As he had said, Rathbone could be found if necessary. Somewhere he had to cash those cheques, somewhere to carry on his queer unhealthy existence. So Carolus made no protest. At the front door Rathbone turned. "I didn't murder Annie," he said. "I never harmed her. I was fond of her."

Then slowly he opened the door and stepped into the sparkling night. Carolus heard the click of the gate, surely the sound which had woken him from sleep an eventful hour ago. He bolted the front door, but before going back to bed he pulled out his handkerchief and very carefully picked up the glass which Rathbone had held and which would show a splendid impression of his fingerprints. He would send that tomorrow to Gillick.

6

In those days at Bluefield Carolus heard recollections of the Rathbones from a number of people and, although not many of these were new, here and there was a fact or a detail which had significance.

The Rector, a splendid chap with a large pipe, had been up at Oxford with Carolus, though they had not met. Mr Lygnett had rowed in the University boat and was altogether a very virile and rather loud-voiced man. "'Fraid I'm a bit intolerant," he explained to Carolus. "I had better say right out that I couldn't stand the fellow. Slinking, effeminate cad . . ."

"Effeminate?" asked Carolus. The word signified for him something he had not associated with Rathbone.

"Yes. I don't mean one of these dressed-up, mincing little rats you see in the West End of London. Make me sick. But there was a sort of softness or weakness in that fellow Rathbone's face which was nearly as bad."

Carolus nodded, seeing what the Rector meant.

"And grubby. Don't believe he took a bath more than once a week. Filthy teeth . . ."

"Really?"

"Nobody need go about with gaps in their teeth today. National Health has stopped that. Must have been just laziness. Revolting character. Sorry if I seem unchristian."

"What about Mrs Rathbone?"

"Poor woman! I don't think he let her out very often. She used to come to church on Sundays. Always crept in late and was gone before we had finished the last hymn. Sat at the back."

"Did you talk to her at all?"

"Never had a chance. I went out to call, but that slimy brute was most offensive. Wouldn't have his wife run after by priests, he said. I'd have knocked him down if he hadn't been such a weed."

"They never came to any village functions?"

"Gracious me, no! We scarcely ever saw them. I don't know whether the Doc was called out there. You could see him, if you like. Lives at that white house almost next door to the Stag."

Carolus went to see Dr Chatto, but with no more satisfactory result. The doctor was a dressy little man with birdlike perkiness, but plenty of intelligence, Carolus thought.

"No, I was never called to the house," he said. "Mrs Rathbone appeared to have excellent health. The man came to the surgery once—some stomach disorder. I told him to have his teeth attended to, eat less tinned food and get some good fresh milk. He admitted that they used tinned milk only."

"Perhaps they didn't want tradesmen calling."

"Very likely. Rathbone never came back to me."

"Did you notice anything about him physically which might help me to piece together this affair?"

"Let me think. Yes, his hands. Extraordinary thing. The man neglected his teeth and looked generally pretty seedy, but he had small, well-kept hands which looked as though they were powerful, too. There was something rather clawlike about them."

Carolus nodded. He always appreciated observation in others.

"Pity you never had to examine Mrs Rathbone," he said. "I might have something to go on then."

"I saw her once or twice. She was a tall, heavy woman. She wore ear-rings and had a nervous trick of smiling."

"Oh. It was a nervous trick?"

"It must have been. One never saw her without that toothy smile."

Carolus thanked Dr Chatto and went to see the only trades-man known to have called at Glose Cottage, a coal-merchant called Toffins. This was a cheery little man who worked from the goods yard of Bluefield station with an ancient lorry. He was assisted by a herculean son.

"Yes," he said, "I knew Rathbone and his wife. Had all their coal from me ever since they came here. It would have made you laugh."

"Why?" asked Carolus, who had not yet got into Mr Toffins' idiom.

"To have seen one or the other, I mean. Him looking like a funeral but having a word with you now and again, and her cheer-ful as could be but never saying more than 'good morning' as she handed over the key of the coal shed. I could have died laughing."

"Did they use much coal?"

"From all accounts it was all they did use much of. I was the only one round here that supplied them with anything. Used to make me smile to think Wallbright and them never got a ha'penny of custom out of them and I supplied them regular. They kept fires on all the time. Must have been the damp. But that always was a cold house."

"Did they have much coal lately?"

"That's what I was just going to tell you. About a month ago, it was, Rathbone came running into my yard as though he'd seen a ghost. You'd have bust yourself laughing. 'Mr Toffins,' he said, 'I'm nearly out of coal. I'd no idea we was so low.' 'All right, all right,' I said to him. 'You can have some tomorrow. How much do you want?' He seemed to calm down a bit then, and thought he'd like a ton. 'You shall have it tomorrow,' I told him, and he

went off. But you should have seen his face. Laugh? I thought I
should never stop."

"Very amusing," said Carolus politely. "How did he pay for
his supplies?"

"By cheque. Always by cheque to Bearer. On his bank at
Folkestone. The Westlay's and Metropolitan."

"Do you remember how the cheques were signed?"

"Yes. By both of them. Her name was on top, 'Anne Rathbone', then his 'Brigham Rathbone'. I remember because Mr Smith
the cashier remarked on it. 'Brigham,' he said, 'that's an unusual
name. Same as the founder of the Mormons.' 'Perhaps he is a
Mormon,' I said, and you ought to have heard us. I thought I
should die laughing."

"You should meet Mrs Gorringer," murmured Carolus.

"Eh?"

"I was going to ask you whether you ever saw anyone else
out at Glose Cottage?"

"Never, in all the times I've been out there."

"What about their dustbin? How did they manage for that?"

"Oh, the lorry only comes round once a month out here. I
don't know what we pay rates for, really. But old George Body,
who collected from them, said they didn't have much. Used to
bury it, he said. He never had a lot to do with them. Well, he'd
tell you the same as what I have."

"Where is the local refuse dumped?"

"Down a disused mine shaft out at Grayfield. Very handy
for this district. Oh, yes, I've often smiled over the Rathbones.
Queer old pair. I said to my son: 'It's a good thing they're not all
like Rathbones, otherwise I shouldn't be able to do my rounds
for laughing.'"

"Quite. You must have a merry life, Mr Toffins."

"Well, there's no sense in going about like a funeral, is there?
I like a good laugh."

"I dare say you had one when you heard the Rathbones
had left."

"It is rather funny, isn't it? Popping off like that. After all the time they've been here. There you are, you never know, do you?"

"You don't," agreed Carolus, and left Mr Toffins to his merriment.

His next and his most important call took him to London, to the offices of Messrs Mumble, Gray & Mumford in Booty Street, Bloomsbury. Carolus realized that he would be on difficult ground here, for solicitors are rightly chary about giving information of any kind, and in a case like this would be doubly so. However, he could only try, and it might be that Mr Mumford would be more communicative than most of his profession.

He found Booty Street a wide but somewhat grey and forbidding thoroughfare near the Gray's Inn Road, and the firm's offices on the first floor of a grim old house. An ancient clerk looked up myopically and Carolus asked for Mr Mumford.

"Have you got an appointment?" said the old man in a voice unexpectedly quick and snappy as he blinked at Carolus.

"No. You might say that I come from Mrs Chalk."

"Mr Mumford's engaged at the moment. I'll find out if he can see you."

It was half an hour before Carolus was shown in to meet a solidly-built, grey-haired man with thin lips and a mechanical smile which was switched on and off apparently at fixed intervals.

Carolus explained his business.

"I'm afraid I couldn't go into that," said Mr Mumford. His smile came on and off like an electric sign.

"I want no breach of confidence, of course," Carolus explained, "but there are one or two things which I think you could tell me quite properly. For instance, is it a fact that Mrs Rathbone was in this office some weeks ago?"

Mr Mumford considered, then said briefly, "It is a fact."

"I think I ought to explain that there is the gravest doubt as to whether the woman who has been living with Rathbone at Bluefield was his wife at all."

Mr Mumford smiled, but it may have been only the periodic lip-stretch.

"Mrs Chalk said something of the kind. It seemed preposterous to me."

"The woman at Bluefield was tall."

"Mr Deene, if you had listened to evidence in court as often as I have, you would not take much notice of witnesses' evidence of height. Mrs Rathbone was short. I understand from Mrs Chalk that she was rarely seen in Bluefield except in her car. That accounts for the discrepancy."

"Not altogether. Did you know Mrs Rathbone?"

"I met her some weeks ago."

"You did not know her at the time she married Rathbone?"

"No, but my father met her at least once when he was dealing with Mr Bright's will. And Potter knew her."

"You'll pardon me, but if that is the gentleman I met in the outer office, do you think his eyesight is to be relied on?"

Smile on. "Yes." Smile off. "I most certainly do. Very shrewd, old Potter. He recognized even her voice. No doubt about it at all. Besides she has been signing her receipts until . . . recently."

"Had she an almost fixed smile?"

"Certainly not. There was nothing eccentric about Mrs Rathbone."

"Except her disposal of an adequate income for life for a lump sum."

"If there was anything of the sort," said Mr Mumford, "I should not be prepared to discuss it."

"I quite understand. But you could, I think, give me the address in Hastings at which Mr. and Mrs Rathbone lived for some years."

"I hardly think . . ."

"Look, Mr Mumford, this woman, or at any rate a woman has disappeared. Possibly two women. I have been asked by Mrs Chalk, a member of the family . . ."

"By marriage, Mr Deene. Only by marriage. We must remember that."

"An interested party at all events. I have been asked by Mrs Chalk to trace her cousin. Surely a three-year-old address, if it is going to aid me, is a small piece of information to ask?"

The inevitable answer came: "It's the principle of the thing. However, on consideration, I see no reason to deny it you. It was 47, Balaclava Grove."

"Thank you. And the address in Bolderton—though I can get that from Mrs Chalk."

"It was Coleshill Lodge, Bolderton. Now is there anything else, because I have a client waiting for me?"

"Yes. Do you know anything of the antecedents of Rathbone? After all, he isn't a client of yours."

"I can give you the name of the firm he worked for before he married our client's daughter. I see no harm in that."

"That is fifteen years ago?"

"Approximately. Yes."

Mumford rang and asked his clerk for the necessary information.

"And now," he said, "let me ask you a question. Do you see any prospect of tracing the Rathbones whom you insist on describing as 'missing'?"

"I have spoken to Rathbone."

"You have?" Smile on. "What is his explanation?" Smile off.

"I scarcely think . . . I am acting in a professional capacity . . ."

"Quite, quite," said Mr Mumford, hoist with his own petard. "You don't think there could be anything er . . . questionable about Mrs Rathbone's . . .er . . . whereabouts?"

"You mean, has she been murdered?"

"Oh, come now, Mr. Deene. Don't let us be melodramatic. People are not murdered."

"No? Perhaps you're right."

"I have never heard anything about the daughter of our client Herbert Bright or about her husband to suggest any impropriety."

"You should go down to the village where they lived. You would hear enough there."

"Gossip? Scandal?"

"No one in the place doubts that Rathbone killed his wife and buried her in the garden or somewhere."

"And you?"

"I don't think she is buried in the garden."

"This is all very disturbing. This firm has never been connected with anything of the sort."

Potter entered and handed Mumford a slip of paper.

"This is the firm for which Rathbone worked before his marriage," he said, and passed the paper to Carolus, who read Tonkins Sons & Company, Wholesale Chemists, 17, Skye Street, Hammersmith.

"They are still there," said Potter quietly.

"Thank you. That is most helpful."

"I trust you will keep us informed," said Mumford. Smile on. "We have a natural interest in the matter." Smile off.

"Another question," said Carolus unhurriedly, but before Potter could leave the room. "Did the Rathbones come to this office during the time they lived at Hastings?"

"My father was alive then and I had no concern with this. Did they, Potter?"

"Several times, Mr Mumford."

"And what was Mrs Rathbone's height then?" asked Carolus. Potter looked pained.

"Just as it always was, of course. She was a short lady. She was ill when they moved to Hastings, I believe, but soon recovered there. She came up a couple of years after their move. She looked very well, I thought."

"The sea air," reflected Carolus.

"Yes," went on Potter. "We remarked on it at the time. She seemed to have quite blossomed out. I remember the late Mr Mumble saying that he ought to move to Hastings. It's a pity he didn't. He might have been alive to this day."

"Come, Potter. Mr Mumble was eighty-one when I joined the firm."

"He might have lived much longer than he did," corrected Potter. "Mrs Rathbone was a delicate lady till she went to Hastings."

"She had a sister, I believe," Carolus threw out, not daring to ask a flat question.

"Dead," said Mr Mumford. Smile on. "Tragic case." Smile off. "We were involved. I have often thought it hastened my father's end."

"What were the details?"

"Most unsavory. She was a woman of . . .er . . . easy morals . . ."

"A woman of the town," put in Potter more explicitly.

"I fear, yes. A . . . er . . . *fille de joie* . . ."

"You mean she was a whore?" said Carolus impatiently.

"In biblical terms, yes. That would be no exaggeration. She was found dead in a miserable room not half a mile from where we are sitting. In an . . . apartment house kept by a Maltese or Cypriot. I never knew which. The only evidence of her identity was a letter from us, advising her some years previously that her father had left her—generously, in view of the circumstances—one thousand pounds."

"So one of you went down?"

"No. No. Quite out of our sphere. We gave the police the address of her sister at Hastings and Mrs Rathbone identified the body."

"When, exactly, was this?"

Mumford glanced at Potter.

"Five years ago, almost to a day," said Potter. "Mrs Rathbone called here afterwards and it was the last time we saw her until she came in the other day in the matter of . . ."

"That will do, thank you, Potter. I have already explained to Mr Deene that if Mrs Rathbone *did* make any new financial arrangements we could not in any case discuss them."

"So the sister died five years ago. Could you give me the address of this apartment house in which she was found?"

"I see no reason against it. Potter?"

"I'll turn it up, Mr Mumford. We found that the name under which she had been work . . . living was Lucille French. She was apparently known among her associates as 'Frenchy'. Women of that calling rarely use their own names."

"You are very well informed."

Potter left the room and came back with the address.

"Here you are. 16b, Montgolfier Street, Flat 27. The proprietor was known as 'Daddy'. He lived in Grosvenor Square. That is the address. His name is Makroides."

"You're most kind."

"I cannot quite see what the circumstances of her unfortunate sister's death have to do with the . . . er . . . absence of Mrs Rathbone," observed Mumford.

"Nor, quite frankly, can I," said Carolus cheerfully; "but it's all grist to the mill. Did Rathbone come up from Hastings with his wife when she had to identify her sister?"

"Certainly. He was reputed to be a most affectionate husband."

"One final question. I take it there was nothing in the circumstances of Charlotte's death to give rise to question?"

Mr Mumford shrugged. "A doctor gave a death certificate," he said; "but with women of that kind I dare say no very searching examination is made or needed. Mrs Rathbone paid for the cremation. You seem to be landing yourself in deep waters, if I may say so, Mr Deene."

"Deeper and deeper," said Carolus.

"What surprises me, if you sincerely intended to find the Rathbones, is that you do not appear to look for them. Instead of going forward you go back into the past."

"Sorry if I sound enigmatic or something," said Carolus; "but in this case the only way to go forward *is* to go back."

Then, after a final expression of thanks, he left the gloomy purlieus of Booty Street.

7

BACK at Bluefield Carolus decided to stop at the Stag for a drink before going out to Glose Cottage. Mr Lofting greeted him like a brother, then leaned across the bar to give him some confidential information.

"The police have been out at your place today," he said. "Digging, I understand. I suppose they're looking for the remains of Mrs Rathbone. I know the chap in charge. A detective sergeant called Cromarty. Damned good scout. An Old Hucknall-Torkardian."

The earlier part of this information was confirmed by Mrs Luggett when she stumped in and dropped gasping in a chair.

"I wouldn't let them into the house, though, till you came. They said they'd got an order and I said so had I—orders not to let anyone in. I never liked policemen and I wasn't going to have them tramping all over the place just when I've begun to get it a bit presentable. So they've been messing about in the garden all day, digging holes and that."

"Did they find anything?"

"Not so far as I know, and I was keeping a pretty sharp look-out on them. They say they'll be there again tomorrow."

"I'm afraid we can't prevent them searching the interior," said Carolus.

"That's up to you. I wasn't going to let them, anyway."

Carolus was awakened next morning by the sound of digging, and looked out to see two burly men turning the soil over while a third in a raincoat looked on. This was presumably Detective Sergeant Cromarty, described by Mr Lofting as a damned good scout. While he was having his breakfast before a blazing fire in the dining-room, this officer was shown in. Carolus saw, only too plainly, what Mr Lofting had meant.

"Sorry about this," said Cromarty in a man-to-man way. "I'm afraid we're making a bit of a shambles of the garden."

"Not at all," said Carolus. "I enjoy nothing more than to see the police at work. Have some coffee?"

"Thanks. Ectually we've nearly finished outside."

"Find anything?"

"I suppose I oughtn't to discuss it, but no. Not up to date."

"Tried the rubbish-heap?"

"Been through it with a fine comb."

"And *under* it?"

Carolus saw that this had gone home. "We shall come to that," said Cromarty casually. "Then I'm afraid we've got to start on the house. Naturally we've got a search-warrant."

"All right with me."

"I was going to suggest that you might like to move out for a few days."

"No thanks."

"I'm afraid we shall produce chaos, rather."

"Can't be helped."

"Floorboards up, perhaps. Wouldn't you be better at the Stag for a bit?"

"Very good of you. But no."

"You see, I can't ectually insist . . ."

"Insist on what?"

"On your moving out. On the other hand we've got our job to do."

"Quite. It will be a unique opportunity to study the methods you learnt on those courses."

"I don't know what to say," said Cromarty uncomfortably. "What is your business, Mr . . . ?"

"Deene. I'm a private investigator."

"You mean you're ectually concerned in this matter of the Rathbones?"

"I can't think of anything else that would induce me to occupy this house."

"This is . . . I scarcely know . . ."

"Why not ask your inspector?"

"We can't have someone hanging round while we conduct a search. Particularly someone interested."

"Awkward, isn't it? On the other hand I'm in occupation of this house. Rented it."

"I see that; but it practically amounts to obstructing the police."

"You exaggerate. I've told you that I welcome your search. There's a most unpleasant smell in the house. I wouldn't think of obstructing you."

Detective Sergeant Cromarty returned to his diggers. From the bedroom window Carolus saw him direct them to remove the pile of rubbish from its corner. One of them seemed to protest mildly, perhaps pointing out that they had done so once. But they fell to and, when the rubbish was gone, showing finely manured earth undisturbed beneath it, Cromarty told them to dig this. Not for a moment did Carolus leave his place of concealment while this was going on, and he was rewarded by seeing one of the men stoop to recover something and hand it to Cromarty. Clearly Carolus could see that it was a gold or gilt ear-ring.

Standing with it in his palm, Cromarty seemed suddenly to remember Carolus, and looked across to see if he was being watched. The temptation was too much for Carolus. He opened the window. "You'll probably find the other one there," he said affably.

Cromarty was not amused. "I don't need you to tell me that," he said, and indicated to the two men that they should dig on. Presently one of them stooped again. The pair of ear-rings was complete.

When it was time for the three policemen to come into the house, Mrs Luggett stood squarely in the back doorway, almost filling it. "You wipe your feet on that scraper," she said. "I'm not having all that mud on my clean lino. You may be able to search, but you can't do what you like in other people's houses." She admitted them after an inspection of their boots and, making straight for the drawing-room, they locked the door behind them.

"That's the kind," Mrs Luggett said to Carolus, explaining her hostility, "that go into Court and swear anyone was drunk and disorderly when all I'd had was a couple of pints of mild. That's the kind that take their oath you was singing at the top of your voice and waking all the neighbors when I'd done no more than hum a bit of *Annie Laurie* as I walked home."

There was a crash from the drawing-room.

"Whatever are they doing in there?" asked Mrs Luggett. "I had that carpet right out the back yesterday, now they'll go and tramp all over it. It isn't right, you know. And what do they expect to find? I suppose they think there's a skelington under the floor. Hark at that! That sounds as though one of the chairs had gone over."

"I tell you what," said Carolus consolingly. "We'll have a little Scotch while they're busy."

"I didn't know you had any," said Mrs Luggett rather too quickly and eagerly.

"Yes. I brought a bottle down last night."

"Oh, I see," said Mrs Luggett. She was clearly relieved. She had been afraid that it had lain undiscovered in the house during Carolus's absence in London yesterday.

"Will you have one, Mrs Luggett?"

"I don't mind. You need something to keep you going, with them doing I don't know what in my clean droring-room. Cheerio, then."

They were interrupted by Fred Spender with the post. Carolus was pleased to see a fairly bulky letter from Battersea, and knew that Gillick's report on the fingerprints, the ashes and the dust from the dressing-table had arrived.

When Mrs Luggett had drunk, said: "That's better", and gone out to the kitchen, Carolus opened the envelope. He found a lengthy report using a good deal of technical phraseology. The house, it seemed, had probably been wiped almost clear of fingerprints before Carolus had occupied it, trouble being taken by someone who had spent time in wiping and polishing every likely surface. In fact the first print that Gillick found was one of Carolus's own, and for a long time he had feared that he might find no other. But, expert in finding prints in places likely to be overlooked by someone deliberately wiping them out, Gillick had eventually discovered three. All were from the same hand, and that hand was the one which had held the glass sent by Carolus—in other words the hand of Rathbone. (Gillick congratulated Carolus on securing this very clear set.) There were no fingerprints discoverable in the house from any other hand. Gillick found nothing extraordinary in this. He did not know how much Carolus had studied the subject, but he would remind him that an ordinary print on a polished surface lasted at the most twenty-four hours, while one on a good surface like that of a looking-glass might be recognizable after three days. The only prints he had expected to find in the house were those left by someone with oily or greasy fingers which would last for weeks. Normally in any house such prints were to be found in the bathroom or kitchen, but in this case there had been a deliberate attempt to clean them up.

The ashes came from coal fires, probably lighted with wood. There was no trace among them of anything such as Gillick presumed Carolus expected to find. No bones or flesh had been burnt in these fireplaces during the time the ash had fallen. But there was evidence of a considerable quantity of cloth having been burnt and, most interesting, a pair of shoes. Gillick had recovered bootmaker's small nails sufficient for at least one pair as well as other evidence that leather had been burnt. Of the dust from the crack in the dressing-table Gillick said simply that it contained a considerable quantity of face-powder.

Immersed in these details, Carolus had not noticed that noises from the drawing-room had ceased. He looked up to see the face of that "good scout" Detective Sergeant Cromarty in the doorway.

"We want to come in here now," he said.

"Well, you can't!" said Mrs Luggett, appearing in the doorway behind him, "because I'm just going to give the gent his dinner and he doesn't want you kicking up the dust while he's eating. I suppose," she went on, obscurely so far as the policemen were concerned, "I suppose you're going to put your hand on the Bible and swear someone couldn't walk and had to be assisted when all I'd had was a small port-and-lemon on Christmas Eve? That's what you'd like to do, I dare say. I know your sort."

"We could do the bedroom first," said Cromarty to Carolus, and so it was arranged.

"You should just see how they've left my droring-room after I Did It Out yesterday! But what can you expect? Assisted! I should like to see one of them trying to assist me. I'd give him some assistance he wouldn't forget. Saying anyone was reeling all over the place and knocking on doors when I never done such a thing in my life! They'd swear your life away, some of them."

It was not until the next morning when some floorboards had been taken up in the entrance passage that another cause of The Smell was discovered. A rat had died there; probably, Carolus told Mrs Luggett, of old age.

Carolus was fairly certain that nothing of any interest had been found by the police. He had himself searched the rooms, and beyond the ear-rings the garden had yielded nothing.

"Of course," he said mischievously to Cromarty, "there's the cement floor of the garage. It looks newly laid to me. Then there's the coal-shed. The coal has only been put in recently."

These gave Cromarty's two assistants a few hours of healthy exercise but revealed nothing. Carolus felt it was time to leave Bluefield. He was unlikely to hear any more of interest and he had seen all he wanted of Glose Cottage. There were other lines of inquiry which he was anxious to follow. He told Mrs Luggett that he would be leaving on the following day, and she accepted this philosophically.

"I was afraid you might, as soon as ever I saw those coppers nosing round. No one's going to stay where they start looking under the bed every five minutes. I shall be sorry in a way. I can get *work*, but it's not everything that suits me. Besides, I've got my own place to look after. Of course, I've got my pension from my husband, but it doesn't go very far. Will you be coming back?"

"I dare say I shall have to."

"I'll pop in tomorrow then and see you off. But I dare say you'll be in at the Stag this evening?"

"Yes."

He did not reach the little bar until nearly nine o'clock and found it crowded. He was surprised at the number of customers he had met in his short stay. There were Mrs Luggett herself, Fred Spender, Mr Toffins and his large silent son, while in a corner in solitary dignity sat Mr Wallbright, the postmaster.

"Well, how did you get on with old Cromarty?" asked Mr Lofting breezily.

"Not well," said Carolus.

"Not? Pity that. Plays cricket for our team here. His mother lives in the village. I saw him knock up a dam' fine 82 last summer on a wicked pitch."

Carolus ordered his drink.

"Perhaps that's where I've met you," reflected Mr Lofting. "Do you go to the Canterbury Week?"

"I'm afraid I don't know what it is."

Mr Lofting laughed. Carolus's disclaimer was not to be taken seriously.

Carolus went over to greet Mr Wallbright, who looked as though he was overcome with mourning the tragic fate of all mankind.

"I've been told," he said after a minute or two, "that you're trying to find out what has happened to the Rathbones."

"Yes."

"I could tell you something, only it's against regulations."

"Pity!"

"If I could be sure it wouldn't be repeated . . ."

"You mean, a letter has come for them?"

"For her, yes. Came this morning. I shall have to send it back 'Gone Away. Address Unknown.'"

"I suppose you will."

"It'll go back to the sender if there's an address in it. If not to the Dead Letter Office."

"That sounds very suitable."

"You mean she's no longer alive?"

"It depends whom we mean by 'she'. I must go over and talk to Mr Toffins."

He found the coal-merchant in the throes of laughter.

"I was just saying to Fred here," he said, controlling himself, "it makes you split your sides to think of those coppers digging up all that garden and not finding anything."

"What did you expect them to find?"

"Her, of course. What do you think? What else were they digging for?"

"That, I take it, would have been an even greater joke?"

"I don't know about that," said Mr Toffins. "I like to think of them doing all that work for nothing."

"I see."

"Moving all that coal! I bet they were black as chimney-sweeps when they'd finished. It tickles me. I could have told them she wasn't under there because she gave me the cheque for it when we'd finished."

"You're sure about that?"

"Quite sure. I remember saying to my son, I wonder where the old man's gone, because it was him opened the door when we first arrived."

"That's very funny," said Carolus.

"I don't see anything funny about that," regretted Mr Toffins.

When he drove out of Bluefield next morning, Carolus hoped that he would not have to return. Almost the only pleasant thing in the village was the gross and bubbling personality of Mrs Luggett. In Grimsgate he returned the keys to Mr Drubbing, who whispered a secretive inquiry. "Not satisfactory?"

"Most. But I have had as much as I wanted."

"Between you and me, I feared you might not stay. It isn't a cheerful house, is it?"

Carolus was delighted to enter his own comfortable home in Newminster, even if he had to find some explanations for Mrs Stick.

"There's been several inquiries," she said when she brought in his tea. "I had to say I didn't know when you'd be back."

"Well, here I am," said Carolus with cheerful fatuity.

"I can only hope you're going to stay, sir," said Mrs Stick.

"I'm afraid that's not possible just at present. I need some sea air, Mrs Stick."

"You've always said Newminster was so healthy."

"No. No. Hastings is the place. Strongly recommended. I leave tomorrow."

"I don't know what to think, I'm sure. I said to Stick last night, one doesn't know what to think, does one? Of course, if it really is a blow of sea air you want and not anything else, I'm sure we should be the last to say anything. But whenever you get down to the sea something always seems to happen. Look at that time down at Oldhaven when you nearly got yourself murdered! And what about Blessington-on-Sea when those bodies kept turning up? I don't know that Hastings will be any better."

"I'm sure the whole Corporation would reassure you, Mrs Stick."

"We can only hope for the best, can't we? I must go and see about your dinner. I'm glad you sent me that telegram this morning or we shouldn't have had anything in. I've got some nice rizzdy vow."

"*What?*" asked Carolus, genuinely baffled.

"Sweetbreads," said Mrs Stick severely, and left him.

8

BALACLAVA GROVE, as its name suggested, was a row of small houses built just after the Crimean War. Apartments were let in some of them, others were unplacarded. They were overshadowed by the high walls of a large commercial hotel which backed on to them.

Carolus found number 47 but, instead of ringing its bell, tried that of the number 45 next door. After he had waited some time, the door was opened a few inches and a feminine face became partially visible.

"I wanted to make an inquiry," began Carolus.

"We don't answer opinion polls. My husband says it's a waste of time."

"It wasn't that . . ."

"We never buy at the door."

"I assure you . . ."

"We don't believe in hire-purchase."

"No. No. It's just . . ."

"Besides, we get all our things from the Co-Op."

"I dare say. I . . ."

"Well, what *do* you want? I'm doing my ironing."

"I wished to inquire about some people called Rathbone who lived at 47 next door."

"How long ago?"

"About three years."

"We've only been here since the summer."

"I see. I'm sorry."

But the door did not shut.

"I tell you what."

Carolus waited.

"The lady on the other side, number 49, might be able to tell you something. She's been here a long time."

"Thank you."

It was always the same. Once the flood-gates were open, there was no stopping the flow. The door remained almost closed, but the voice continued:

"If not, them in the house now, number 47 I mean, ought to know something."

"Yes. I'll inquire."

"Of course, you could always go to the police station."

"Quite."

"But the lady at 49 would know. She's been here a good many years." The dark inquisitive eyes continued to stare from the obscurity behind the door. "You'll find her at home now. She doesn't go out till the afternoon."

"It's very kind of you."

"You want to give a good knock because she may be right upstairs."

"Of course."

"I expect she knew these you're talking about. She seems to know everything."

"Yes."

"I don't say she's nosy, mind you, but she's lived here a long time."

There was only one thing to be done, Carolus decided. He must forget his manners and simply walk away. He gave a quick nod and went. As he knocked at Number 49, however, the face which had remained hidden obtruded from the doorway of Number 45.

"That's right," his late informant said, "give a good knock. She'll be down in a minute." It was evident that she intended to see the meeting she had suggested safely made. "I should knock again if I was you; she may be out the back." Carolus did.

"She ought really to have a bell, like we've got. It's awkward, waiting about, isn't it?" It was, watched by those dark eyes.

"I'm sure she's not out. I should have seen her go. She always comes by this way." Carolus waited.

"You can't hear the dog barking, can you?"

Just then the door of Number 49 was flung open wide and Carolus faced its occupant. Miss Ramble was a sinewy person with an ochreous complexion and chaotic clothes. Carolus had the impression—he thought afterwards that he must have been mistaken—of lace round the thin neck and a display of old-fashioned jewellery. There was a sort of aqueous fire in the eyes and altogether too much fluttering movement.

"Oh, good morning," began Carolus. "I have a small favor to ask. I believe you may have been acquainted with some people called Rathbone."

Miss Ramble looked Carolus in the eyes, then with a gesture said: "Come in!"

He was shown, ushered rather, into a room which made him gape. It could not have been arranged, he realized, for a joke or a film set, it must be real. There were pampas grass and antimacassars, beadwork foot-stools and papier-mâché tables; there were ornamental china and plush curtains, wallpaper with pink lilies-of-the-valley threaded by green ribbon with bunches of yellow violets; there was a picture-rail from which hung by copper wire a selection of mezzotint engravings of the works of Lord Leighton and Holman Hunt; there was a crocheted tablecloth over a plush one and there was an ebonized upright piano.

"Sit down!" cried Miss Ramble, indicating with a sweeping gesture a *chaise-longue* covered in a patchwork. "The Rathbones? Indeed I was acquainted with them. It seems only yesterday that they were in this room. We were, for a time, something more than neighbors."

"Only for a time?"

"Yes. Towards the end there was a rift. I blame myself for giving confidence too readily. My weakness. But tell me, why do you come to inquire from me about the Rathbones?"

"They have disappeared."

Miss Ramble received this as though it were a shock, violently jerking back her head. "Terrible! You mean they have absconded?"

"I don't know. A relative of Mrs Rathbone's has asked me to trace them. So I have come to you."

"But," said Miss Ramble, her every word spoken with emotion and emphasis, "it is three years since I saw them!"

"Yes. Still, I would ask you, if you will, to remember what you can about them. It will certainly help. Could you, for instance, describe them?"

"I could! He was of middle height, with a small moustache. His hair was greying and there was a strange watchfulness in his rather melancholy eyes. It was not a handsome or a forceful face."

"And Mrs Rathbone?"

"She was a dumpy little thing."

"Little?"

"*Petite.*"

"And stout?"

"Plump."

"Did she smile often?"

"She had a very cheerful disposition and laughed easily, but I don't think she smiled particularly often."

"You describe them very well. I should like you just to go on telling me what you remember of them as it comes to you."

"I will. They lived next door for about three years. They were Christian Scientists."

"Really?"

"Oh, yes. Don't you know that? When they arrived here, Mrs Rathbone was so ill that she had to be carried into the house from the motor-car. For many weeks she was not seen, but her husband cared for her so well that, when she at last emerged, she seemed in excellent health. Thereafter, while they were here, neither of them had a day's illness. I was impressed. I asked them about their religion, but they did not seem anxious to discuss it, and referred me to a Christian Science Reading Room, where my interest wilted and died."

"So they never called a doctor?"

"Never. It was against their principles."

"Was there anything of the recluse about them?"

"Not in the least. On the contrary, Mrs Rathbone was most sociable and her husband seemed to enjoy our little occasions of merriment in his quiet way. My Voice had not then deserted me and many was the evening when I rendered them the 'songs and snatches' of my earlier days. It was, in fact, over one such occasion that our memorable rift occurred."

"How was that?"

"I cannot bear vulgarity. The witty, the lively, even, within reason, the risqué, I will accept, but vulgarity, no! One evening Mrs Rathbone suddenly rendered a song at the piano which I blush to remember. I felt bound to tell her that it was offensive to me and she laughed in a very coarse way and made a quite unforgivable remark. I asked them to leave the house."

"That was towards the end of their stay here?"

"Within six months of it, I should say. I bore them no ill will. I realize that to some people I should seem intolerant. But life is too beautiful a thing to be cheapened by vulgarity. You may smoke if you wish."

"Thank you. This was the first time that anything of the sort had occurred?"

"With me, yes. But I had heard Talk."

"Talk?"

"Mrs Rathbone was not, I fear, quite what I should call a lady. Her manner of dress and her bearing left something to be desired. Although I myself saw no sign of it, for she would scarcely reveal such a thing to me, there was a rumor that she sometimes drank more than was good for her. I do not listen to gossip, but I could not avoid hearing that she went to a certain public house called the Star and Mitre. Certainly there was something rubicund about her which suggested intemperance."

"I see."

"I do not believe she was an ill-intentioned woman. Indeed she was considered affable and friendly. But she lacked refinement."

"Her husband had no occupation while they were here?"

"None. They had private means, I understood. I sometimes thought Mr Rathbone was rather an indolent person."

"Did they ever speak of any relatives?"

"Not when I first knew them. But about a year after they came here, Mrs Rathbone's sister died in London. There was something a little curious about that, because I am *almost* sure they first had the news from a policeman."

"Really?"

"Yes! About four o'clock one day I chanced to be seated near the window. I was catching the last of the light for some *petit-point* embroidery I was doing. I distinctly saw a policeman call at their house. When I met them later that evening, I did not venture to remark on what I had seen, but I detected something uneasy in their manner. Next day they left for London, and on the following day they were absent again. They told me afterwards that they had attended the cremation of Mrs Rathbone's sister. I did then mention the policeman's call and they dismissed this quite peremptorily. To do with their motor-car, they said; but I could not help wondering whether the sister's death had not been . . . irregular, in some way."

"A very natural supposition. And you were quite right. Mrs Rathbone was called to identify her sister's body."

"I feared something of the sort. It is consistent with . . . the Other."

Carolus waited.

"You know, of course, that there was considerable speculation about their manner of leaving here? You don't? Of course it may all be no more than hearsay. I should not wish to repeat mere gossip."

"In a case like this, mere gossip may be of the greatest importance."

"Then I will tell you! The house beyond theirs was then occupied by a very worthy person who let apartments during the summer—a Mrs Bishop. It was from her that I gathered the extraordinary story. How, you may be asking yourself, did I come to associate with her? She was of quite humble origin, but a very well-behaved, respectful woman and I saw no reason to treat her unkindly. She would occasionally come here and stay for a cup of tea. She it was who first told me that there was trouble between the Rathbones. It appeared—she explained this as delicately as possible—it appeared that Mrs Rathbone had formed a liaison with another man. A commercial traveller of some kind, I gathered.

"I did not require all the squalid details. I was thankful that I had put an end to my acquaintance with the Rathbones before this took place; but Mrs Bishop insisted that the two had been seen together on the promenade late at night and that Rathbone was extremely angry about it. This continued for some weeks. I myself saw nothing that could be thought in any way improper, though one evening when I happened to be near my bedroom window a car drew up which was certainly not the Rathbones' car and Mrs Rathbone stepped out of it. I heard her call good night to the occupant of the car before it was driven away. Then she entered her house. In itself nothing, you will say. But wait!"

Carolus waited.

"Three days elapsed, then towards dusk I saw both the Rathbones leaving their house, bearing suitcases. By a coincidence I was just stitching a small tear in my lace curtain at the time.

They placed these suitcases in their car and drove away. From that moment onwards I never saw Mrs Rathbone again!"

Giving Miss Ramble all his attention but not interrupting, Carolus nodded gravely.

"It was some days before I saw Mrs Bishop. She, too, it appeared, had chanced to be glancing from her window when the suitcases were brought out. She said that Rathbone had not returned till late that night and when he came he was alone. She met him in the street the following day and he seemed, in her words, 'very upset'. 'My wife has left me!' he said. Mrs Bishop suggested that of course she would soon be back and he said: 'Yes, yes,' in an abstracted way and walked on. Strange, you will own."

"Well, not necessarily. Wives do leave husbands for other men."

"That was *not* the general interpretation of the circumstances. It was whispered . . . I hesitate to tell you this . . ."

"I dare say I can guess. They said that Rathbone had done away with his wife, I suppose."

"They did! It was quite a scandal in the town. The circumstances were unusual. So sudden, you see."

"How, I wonder, was he supposed to have disposed of the body?"

"That was the mystery; but it was pointed out that there is always the sea. Then someone claimed to know that Rathbone had once been employed by a firm of wholesale chemists. It was suggested that acid might have been used!"

"I wonder why. After all, so far as anyone knew, here was a wife leaving her husband with his full knowledge, if not consent. Why should they have made such sinister suggestions?"

"I think, perhaps, it was something about Rathbone himself. I am not saying that I was a party to these rumors, but I did think, looking back on my acquaintance with him, that Rathbone could have been *that* kind of man. One reads such dreadful cases in the papers."

"I see what you mean."

"However, since as you now tell me the two have been together again . . ."

"I did not quite say that. Rathbone has been living in a lonely part of the country with a woman whose description is quite unlike that you give me of his wife. She has disappeared in much the same circumstances."

"How *very* horrible! The man must be a monster!"

"He left here soon after this happened?"

"Almost immediately. His furniture was removed by a London firm Mrs Bishop regretted afterwards that she had not made a note of the name. We have heard nothing of him or of her from that day to this."

"I am most grateful to you, Miss Ramble. Your information will be very valuable. By the way, did Mrs Rathbone wear earrings?"

"Never!"

"What was her age, would you say?"

"Not more than forty, I should guess."

"And you are certain that she was short and stout?"

"Quite certain."

Carolus rose and took a last regretful look at the room in which they had been sitting. Those Japanese fans! That walnut whatnot! He might never see, in its natural state as it were, such a room again.

"Rubicund, you say?"

"Yes. Even a hint of purple sometimes. Full cheeks; indeed, as I have said, heavy altogether. I remember noticing—though it is not pleasant to discuss such things—that the calves of her legs were unbecomingly solid."

"She never wore glasses?"

"Never. Not even to read music." Miss Ramble seemed to have something more to say but found difficulty in it. "I hesitate to suggest," she began; "I was just wondering . . . if it would not be too much trouble . . . I should be *most* interested to hear what transpires. If you could kindly tell me any developments as they occur . . . Mrs Bishop has moved to Sebastopol Avenue, but we still see one another occasionally and she would be glad to receive any news, too, I know."

Carolus gave some vague assurance and moved to the door. Miss Ramble let him out with a dramatic gesture of farewell. But he had forgotten Number 45, outside which his car still stood. As he passed, its door was opened, this time quite widely.

"You found her all right, then?"

"Yes, thank you."

"I thought you would. She doesn't often go out till the afternoon."

"No."

"Well, I'm glad you found her in."

"Yes."

"You don't want to come and see someone and not find them, do you?"

"No."

"I mean, it's such a nuisance when you've come a long way."

"Yes."

Carolus started his car and with a cheerful wave of his hand left Balaclava Grove behind.

But he was not feeling cheerful. Even more than in the stuffy gloom of Glose Cottage he was filled with a rising sense of disgust. Remembering the shifty face of Rathbone gave him a feeling of physical nausea. He knew instinctively that there would be more to come. Tall and heavy, short and plump—but the original Mrs Rathbone had been described as a skinny little thing. He began to wonder where it would end.

9

CAROLUS had thought it would be necessary to stay in Hastings for some days, for he had not foreseen the dramatic and informative Miss Ramble. He was satisfied that he had the facts he needed but conscientiously determined not to depend on a single witness, and called that evening at the Star and Mitre where the landlord remembered the Rathbones well and confirmed most of Miss Ramble's details. He reached his home after the Sticks had gone to bed, but faced his fiery little housekeeper over breakfast next morning.

"So it *was* you came in last night!" she said. "I was only saying to Stick we weren't to know. It might have been anyone."

Carolus attacked his kedgeree.

"Only we should like to know," said Mrs Stick.

"What?"

"Whether you'll be staying, now you're back. I thought it was the sea air you were going to Hastings for."

"Yes. I shall be staying some time, I think," said Carolus. "But I shan't be in to lunch or dinner today and I may stop tonight in town."

"It's no good my getting anything in, then, is it?" asked Mrs Stick as she left Carolus. She seemed perplexed more than put out, he thought absently, as he picked up *The Times* and turned straight to the crossword.

He knew that he must next go to Bolderton, the place in which the Rathbones had lived before they moved to Hastings. He felt something like dread at the prospect. He was fairly certain that he would hear yet another description of another Mrs Rathbone. But he went. He drove through London without more delay than usual, reflecting that a horse carriage sixty years ago would have covered the distance from Blackheath to Barnet in about a third of the time he took. He found Bolderton a region of new houses, thick with television aerials, busy with self-service shops, humming with motor-scooters. Deep in a maze of almost uniform streets an old high wall still rose, behind which Coleshill, once a lonely manor house, was maintained as a rehabilitation center for juvenile delinquents. It was now called Coleshill College. Much of the manor's grounds had been built over, and what had once been the lodge was separated from the college playing-fields by another row of red-brick family cells named Aneurin Road; but the lodge had miraculously kept its character and square of garden. Between this garden and the road was a row of iron hurdles and shrubs. He felt that Mrs Chalk had exaggerated in calling it a "gloomy little house", but after Glose Cottage he was apt to find any dwelling cheerful by comparison.

A pleasant, middle-aged woman came to the door and answered his questions in a businesslike way. She and her husband had taken the lodge soon after the Rathbones had vacated it. They had never seen the Rathbones, but had heard a good deal about them from Mrs Richards, the char whom they had inherited from the previous occupants. Mrs Richards had remained with them till quite recently, but no longer went out to work. Carolus could find her at 14 Jupp Street, near the station.

"My husband might be able to tell you more than I can," said the lodge's occupant. "He saw the estate agents at the time. I'm sure he would be quite willing to give you any information if it will help to trace someone missing. He gets home about five, but six-thirty would be the best time."

Carolus expressed his thanks and went off to find Mrs Richards, whom he thought rather a pretty old thing, with very white hair and rosy cheeks. She lived with her daughter and son-in-law. Everyone seemed intelligent and helpful, he reflected. There was nothing in the least dim or macabre about Bolderton.

"Oh, yes," said Mrs Richards when she had asked him into the living-room of her daughter's home, "I remember the Rathbones well. I worked for them for some years just after the war. You say they've disappeared? That's what they did from here in a way. They hadn't long been married when they came to Bolderton. They seemed quite comfortably off, but I believe it was her money. Her father had died a year or so before and, though I never heard any details, I think he had left her everything.

"Mr Rathbone was older than his wife. He wasn't what you'd call a healthy-looking man. Rather weedy, I'd say. It really got on my nerves to see him hanging about all day doing nothing. He didn't seem to have any interests, even. He wasn't a man who could turn his hand to anything in the house. Couldn't even fit a new washer on a tap. He'd sit about in slippers all the morning, reading the paper and smoking. I used to have to get him out of his armchair. 'I want to Do this room now, Mr Rathbone,' I'd say, and he'd have to move. But I think he was fond of his wife in a way. There were never any words between them and when she became ill later on he looked after her very attentively. Mrs Rathbone . . ."

"Excuse me," Carolus interrupted. "Would you mind describing her?"

"What she looked like, you mean? There was nothing of her, as you might say. A little peeked thing she was. Very nice to speak to, mind you. Always considerate and that. But very quiet. Rather sad-looking, I always thought. She didn't seem to know how to enjoy herself."

"They didn't go out much?"

"Only to the cinema sometimes. It was before the telly had come in as it has."

"Did either of them drink?"

"He liked a little sometimes. Oh, never too much, but he did pop into the Greyhound now and again. She never did. When the doctor ordered her to have a glass of milk-stout in the mornings it was as much as she could do to swallow it."

"They had the doctor, then?"

"Oh, yes. Dr Whistley it was. He's still in the town if you want to see him. He used to come about once a week to see Mrs Rathbone when she was ill. Pernicious anaemia, they called it. She became a proper invalid and stayed in her room all day. Sometimes she would sit up for an hour or two but you could see it was a strain. At one time it really looked as though she wasn't going to live. They had to send for her sister."

"What was the sister like?"

"I never saw her. She went there one day after I'd come home from work. But the nurse they had at that time told me next morning you'd never have believed she was Mrs Rathbone's sister from the way she behaved. I shouldn't like to repeat what the nurse said about her, but it wasn't very nice. Then, after that, Mrs Rathbone must have been better, because they got rid of the nurse. I never saw much difference in her, ill or well, myself, but then we're a healthy family and, although I've brought up three, I've never had much experience of illness. Mrs Rathbone always looked the same to me, poor thing."

"You said something which suggested that they left suddenly."

"Yes. They did. It was a funny business altogether. I got there one morning at my usual time and found Mr Rathbone down in the kitchen as though he'd been waiting for me. I could see he was upset about something and it came to me he was trying to ask me to leave—after I'd been with them all that time. He said it was the house, it was damp and he was going to take Mrs Rathbone away, down to the sea. I said it might be a good thing. She looked as though that was what she needed. 'She does,' he said, 'I'm going to take her at once. Today if possible; if not, tomorrow. So we shan't need you any more, Mrs Richards.' Of course I was surprised. 'You'll want someone to clear up,' I said. 'No, that doesn't matter. I'll do what's necessary.' Then he tried to be civil. 'Thanks very much for all your help,' he said and gave me three weeks' money. What could I do? But they didn't leave that day nor yet the next. I heard it was three days later when they drove away in the evening. There were no houses just by the Lodge in those days. All those have been built since then. So I don't know who saw them go, but that's what was said. There was a lot of talk about it at the time."

I seem to have heard that before, thought Carolus wearily. But he asked: "What kind of talk?"

"In a place like this there are always those who think the worst. Their getting rid of the nurse and me and going off after dark like that. Some of them went so far as to say that he'd murdered her. But you know what people are when anything happens. They're always ready to talk. I never liked Mr Rathbone very much because I've always been a worker, and it didn't seem right to me that a man should be idle; but I don't believe he would have done his wife any harm. As I say, he seemed very fond of her."

"Afterwards you worked for the next occupants?"

"Mr and Mrs Humbell, yes. They're very nice. I like sticking to the same place, and as soon as I saw their furniture going in I went and offered and started straight away. I was with them quite recently till my daughter wanted me to stay at home. Well, there was no need for me to go out any more. My daughter has a good job and her husband earns wonderful money as he's a skilled carpenter. Besides, someone's got to give the children their dinner in the middle of the day. So I gave it up. But they're very nice people, the Humbells."

"Was the house unoccupied long?"

"Not with the shortage of houses. No sooner was the Rathbones' furniture out of the way . . ."

"They took that?"

"No, sent for it afterwards. I'd like to have gone in and put it straight before the moving men saw it. Clattons had the keys, I believe, the estate agents in the High Street. The Rathbones had only been gone about a week when their furniture was sent for from London. Mr Humbell saw the house next day and took it at once. You couldn't get a place, not to rent, in those days and he thought he was lucky. I always think it's damp, but they've made it very nice inside now. Quite different to what it was when the Rathbones were there."

"So you were only away from the house for a week or ten days, then, between your notice from Rathbone and your starting with the Humbells?"

"It couldn't have been any more."

"Did you notice anything changed in the garden?"

"No. And I had a good look round. The Rathbones took no interest and had a jobbing gardener in once a week. I liked to see what he'd done but, so far as I could notice, there was nothing. It was just as I'd seen it."

Carolus asked Mrs Richards for Dr Whistley's address, thanked her for her assistance and drove to the doctor's. Here he explained to an elderly woman, as intelligent and polite as everyone else in the suburb, that he would like to see Dr Whistley on a private matter. He was shown into a pleasant sitting-room. The doctor was elderly, but quick and shrewd. He looked at Carolus as though impatient to size him up. Carolus wasted no time at all, but told him succinctly the reason for his visit.

"Now that's odd," said Whistley. "I always thought someone would come and ask me about the Rathbones, but I expected it at the time—not years afterwards. It was a curious case. I was treating Mrs Rathbone when quite suddenly they moved away and I was never consulted by any colleague elsewhere."

"She had pernicious anaemia, I believe?"

"Yes. Anaemia should not be considered as a disease in itself. It is rather the symptom of some underlying disorder. This I was trying to discover when the couple suddenly moved away."

"What are the symptoms?"

"They're rather technical and vary from case to case. Mrs Rathbone had several of the classic ones. Her hair was greying rapidly and prematurely. The tongue was smooth and red. Then there was developing a disturbance of the spinal cord which we call combined system disease. She grew very pale with a typical yellowish cast to the skin. She had become listless, in fact was in danger of being crippled."

"Could this be fatal?"

"Like many other diseases, not many years ago it certainly would have been. It was not until the 1920s that the use of liver extracts was properly understood and manufactured for injection purposes. Then, only a year or two before I treated Mrs Rathbone, we began using Vitamin B 12. There was no reason to suppose, in Mrs Rathbone's case, that if she continued this treatment she might not live to an advanced age. On the other hand, as I have explained, I do not know what caused her condition. There may have been something which could produce a very rapid decline and possibly death. She greatly improved with Vitamin B 12, but she was still in a low nervous condition. Almost neurasthenic, in fact."

"Her removal need not have harmed her?"

"No. Not necessarily. Rathbone apparently told people that he was taking his wife to the sea, but he gave me no indication of this. I was seeing her once a week and arrived one morning to find they had left."

"You did not feel it necessary to report the matter?"

"To the police? No. Why should I have? The sudden departure of a man with an invalid wife is not a police affair. I am far too busy to be inquisitive about comings and goings among my patients. I gather there was talk about this at the time, but a GP gets used to talk of that kind."

"Yet you say that you expected inquiries afterwards?"

"Well, yes. Perhaps from a colleague who treated her. You see, that treatment had to be maintained. Otherwise the anaemia would return and perhaps a crippling of the nervous system which might not be curable. I'm afraid I am not being very helpful when all you want is to find these people."

"You are. Most. But my problem is becoming a tough one. I started to look for a Mrs Rathbone who was missing and I now find traces of three of them. Unless the Mrs Rathbone you remember could possibly have become someone described as a 'dumpy', 'plump', 'cheerful', 'most sociable', 'affable' woman, who sang vulgar songs at the piano, drank more than was good for her, had a love affair with a commercial traveller under her husband's nose, was rubicund with 'a hint of purple' in her cheeks and had legs the calves of which were 'unbecomingly solid'."

"Impossible, if the description is reliable."

"Or, on the other hand, could have become 'tall', 'always smiling', 'a bit of a gorgon', 'wearing glasses and old-fashioned clothes', a 'funny old thing', 'old-fashioned-looking', 'a big woman, tall and big-made', 'a funny-looking old crow', 'always had a smile', 'cheery-looking', 'appeared to have excellent health', 'never without a toothy smile'. It doesn't fit very well, does it?"

"It doesn't. But it's the same man each time?"

"Yes. Rathbone."

"I don't like the sound of it. Something like this would have emerged if anyone had started going back over the life of Brides-in-the-Bath Smith, wouldn't it?"

"I suppose so."

"Rathbone was a rather strange being, I remember. But these wife murderers are supposed to be the most ordinary little men."

"So I believe. It's an interesting case, but a nasty one. You never saw Mrs Rathbone's sister, did you?"

"No. I believe she came down once but I was not there."

"Thank you very much, Doctor."

"I should like to hear what you discover."

"I think you will—from any newspaper. If I'm right about this, you won't be able to escape hearing about it."

Before leaving for his club where he intended to stay the night, Carolus returned to the Lodge to meet Mr Humbell, who would by now have returned from work and eaten.

"This is the gentleman I was telling you about," Mrs Humbell said, "who is trying to trace the Rathbones."

Mr Humbell, a sturdy, grey-haired elderly man who looked as though he came from Yorkshire but spoke without dialect, invited Carolus to sit down. "There's not a lot I can tell you," he said. "They had left here before we arrived. I moved our furniture in almost as theirs went out, as you had to in those days. I had the place done up afterwards and it needed it."

"Nothing was left behind, by chance?"

"Absolutely nothing. It was moderately clean, as Mrs Richards had been looking after them until a day or two before they left."

"Yes. I've seen Mrs Richards. And since then you've never come on anything anywhere . . ."

"No. Would you expect it?"

"You see, Mr Humbell, this is the third place I've been to from which the Rathbones moved suddenly and rather mysteriously. One of the others was a house in a town without a garden but at the other, in a lonely part of the country, the police have investigated thoroughly. Dug the garden and everything."

"What did they find?"

"Nothing, I believe, but a pair of ear-rings."

"You're not suggesting that here there may be evidence hidden?"

"I'm past suggesting," said Carolus. "This affair is getting me down. But it was only because a later tenant pulled down a wall, or something, that Christie was discovered."

"Then why haven't the police been here?"

"I don't know, but I imagine the police are going forward, instead of back. Looking for Rathbone and his wife wherever they may be. They are probably quite right. I go about things in my own way. But in time they may trace the Rathbones here and wonder, as I do, whether a search would be worth while."

"Yes. I see. I shall have to think it over."

So, Carolus thought as he drove back to London, so would he. For although he began to see the vague shape of the truth it was ghostlike and elusive. Perhaps if he could trace that woman "Cara" who had lived with Charlotte Bright (known as "Lucille French") it might advance matters. Charlotte could have told her about her visit to Bolderton during her sister's illness, or something else that would be valuable. He still had that address to visit—the house in which "Frenchy" had died.

10

He decided next day to make straight for Montgolfier Street and hope to find someone who remembered Charlotte Bright. He realized that the chances were against him, for the population in such an apartment house would be a shifting one and it was five years since Charlotte's death; but this was the sort of challenge which he enjoyed.

It took him three days to pick up the lightest thread. During that time he inquired of a great variety of people, from Makroides himself to the barman of a pub in Charlotte Street, from ladies with busy telephones to a girl in a lung hospital. He met a good deal of hostility, some ridicule and some unselfish kindness, and he covered considerable distance on foot and by car, largely in regions between Soho and St Pancras. Five years ago seemed to be pre-history to most of those he asked and the apartment house in Montgolfier Street had long since become respectable. The less pleasant part of his search was in arty little clubs, and it was in one of these that he was told off-handedly—"You ought to ask Old Maree. She lived in that house for donkey's years."

More hours of search brought him to "Old Maree" herself and that would have rewarded him even if she could have told him nothing. For "Old Maree" was remarkable.

First, though her hair blazed with a lurid copper color, she *was* old. But not old enough, as she said, to have "crumpled". She sat proudly upright on a straight chair in the little bar she had suggested and said—"Old? I can't afford to be. Though it's surprising how often the young ones get passed over. It's not years or even lines in your face. It's how you stand up. Once you begin to Go you've had it. I remember seeing *No, No Nanette*, so you can see I wasn't born yesterday. But I don't complain.

"I tried to settle down once. I'd always had a fancy for chickens. That'll seem funny to you but, if there's one thing I like, it's a nice fresh egg. So I took this place in the country with another girl. I stuck it six months, then I was back. It's what you get used to. Thanks. I'll just have plain gin.

"So you want to know about poor Frenchy. Well, I can tell you because I had the room next but one to hers in Montgolfier Street. That's all been done away with now. The Law got on to it and that Makroides they used to call Daddy did six months. But it was handy then. Right in the center and no one to interfere with you. Frenchy came to live there after the girl she'd been with went off with a fellow to the country. A girl called Cara. She's still about, because I saw her the other day. Only she doesn't get around the West End any more. She's living steady with a fellow called Myberg. She was a character, was Cara. Anything for a laugh. She told me the other day: 'I'm Mrs Myberg now. What d'you think of that?' Got a place Bayswater way and nicely settled down, she says. I was pleased to see her and we had quite a chat. I asked her if she'd heard about Frenchy and she said: 'Yes, I heard the poor cow was dead.' That's the way she talked, even about anyone Gone. But she didn't mean anything. It was just her way.

"I'd left Montgolfier Street before Frenchy died there, but I heard about it. Nobody seemed to know what the cause of it was. It was quite sudden, though she was never what you might call strong. A long string of a girl, she was, with big dark eyes. You couldn't help noticing her. Long neck and sort of prancing walk. When she used to live with Cara, they got on well together, because they were so different. But Cara went away suddenly with this fellow. Said she was only going to be away for the day, then never came back. Frenchy thought she must have been seeing him for some time on the sly. She never said anything to Frenchy. So Frenchy, who knew me, met me one evening and said Cara had gone off, so did I know of a room she could afford on her own, and I told her about Montgolfier Street. She came round and moved in, and after that I saw quite a lot of her. Only after a time I couldn't afford that place. Makroides used to charge something wicked for the rooms. They all do, but his was the worst of the lot and I moved out. It can't have been more than month later when poor Frenchy was found dead."

"*Found* dead?"

"Yes, well that's what happens. No one's going to disturb you and it may be a day or two before anyone begins to wonder. When they found her, they said she'd been dead the best part of two days. Yes, I don't mind. Just plain gin. I hope I'm not doing all this talking for nothing?"

"No," said Carolus. "You're on to a fiver."

"I should think so. There's no one else could tell you all this. Where was I? Oh, yes, there she was, dead for two days. So they had to find out who she was, didn't they? Lucille French she called herself, but that didn't mean much. So they started going through her things and all they found to identify her was a letter from some lawyer about ten years ago saying her old man had died and left her a thousand nicker. Only that was before I'd known her. I forget her real name. Charlotte something."

"Bright," said Carolus.

"I don't remember that. But I know it was Charlotte because that's a French name, isn't it, and I remember thinking to myself, that's why she took the name French. Oh, well, she's Gone now. Here's cheers." "Old Maree" adjusted herself in the chair she overlapped and squared her shoulders. "One of the girls in the house told me about it, though I don't know how she knew all the details. Must have been friendly with the cops. It seems they got in touch with these lawyers who'd written the letter, but they wouldn't have anything to do with it, and put them on to her sister who was married and lived down at Brighton or somewhere."

"Hastings."

"It may have been. You seem to know more about it than I do. If you know everything, I'd like to know why you're asking me."

"No. I don't. Please go on."

"There's not much more to tell. They'd taken poor Frenchy to the mortuary by then and the sister went there to identify her. After that she was cremated. I shouldn't like that. Would you? Shrivelled up to a couple of cinders. Oh, well. We can't live forever, that's quite sure. Well, just one more, then I must run along. Plain gin."

"So that's all you can tell me about Frenchy?"

"Isn't it enough? She's Gone, so I don't know what more's to be said. If you want to hear more, you better see Cara. Only don't forget she's Mrs Myberg now. She won't want a lot of this brought up again, you can be sure of that. But, if you can get her on her own, she might tell you something. What's it all about?"

"It's not really about Charlotte Bright herself. I'm trying to trace her sister, who has disappeared."

"Oh, that's it! And you think that poor Frenchy might have said something to Cara which would help?"

"Yes. Charlotte, I mean Frenchy, went down to see her sister when she was very ill."

"When was that?"

"About six years ago."

"Cara was living with her then for certain. They were together for years before Frenchy came to Montgolfier Street and that must be nearly that. I can't remember time, not to the year. But you can be sure Cara knew her then. What's the Law doing about it, anyway?"

"I don't really know. I was asked by a relative if I could trace this woman."

"Oh, well. It's a funny life."

"I suppose you haven't got Mrs Myberg's telephone number?"

"No, I haven't. But I should think you'd find it in the telephone book. The way she was dressed and that. I believe this chap she's with is in quite a big way of business."

"I see."

"Well, it looked like it, and Cara wasn't a girl to settle down for nothing, if you know what I mean. Funny how they come and go, isn't it? There's not many of those around today I can say I know. Not to say know. Of course they all know me. There was a journalist chap talking to me the other evening, the cheeky bastard, and he says: 'We all know you, Maree. You're a bit of Old London,' he says, 'like the Old Lady of Threadneedle Street.' 'Who's she?' I asked. 'I bet she hasn't been round longer than I have. And what a pitch! What's she expect to do up there in the evening?' But he only laughed. Well, I'm not ashamed of it. And I keep wonderfully well. That's the gin. Yes, I will have one for the road."

Carolus brought it from the bar.

"As I was saying, it's gin keeps me so well. I always drink it like that, not messed up with water or vermouth or anything. Have done for years. It's the best thing for anything like indigestion. Then I give myself a good eight hours sleep, never mind what time I get to bed. That's another secret. I tell them, I say I shall be still going when you poor cows are pushing up daisies. Here's cheers."

Carolus raised his glass, no longer expecting to hear anything highly pertinent but fascinated by "Old Maree".

"That Cara liked a drink. I've seen her well away. I don't know how she gets on now she's right out there in Bayswater. I suppose she finds somewhere to go. But it seems this Myberg is very jealous. I dare say he knows what she was, as you might say, and keeps a good eye on her. That's a change for her. So did Frenchy like a drink—or Charlotte, as you call her. You say she had a sister. I suppose I wouldn't have known her, would I?"

"I don't think so. She was apparently a rather mousy little person who lived with her father and was married within a year of his death."

"Perhaps that's why I never heard Frenchy speak of her. Here! You see that girl just come in on her own? Her with the violets, I mean; she always wears violets. I don't know how she can afford it. Well, she knew Frenchy. She stayed on at Montgolfier Street after I did. She was there when Frenchy Went. Would you like me to bring her over? Only I don't suppose she'll want to waste a lot of time."

"Please," said Carolus.

The "girl", whose name it appeared was Elizabeth, had a voice that might have been trained in one of those rooms with French windows and sunlight that are found only as the settings for West End comedies. She had an air of great sophistication or, as "Old Maree" said later, she had class. When Carolus asked her what she would have to drink she said: "I suppose Maree's lapping up her old neat gin. I'll have a B and S."

It was from his reading of Lytton Strachey's essay on General Gordon that Carolus had learned the interpretation of this and brought over a brandy and soda.

"Oh, yes, I remember the woman you're discussing," said Elizabeth. "Quite a pleasant type. Murdered, probably."

"How can you talk like that?" said "Old Maree". "You'll give me the creeps for a week. How could she have been murdered?"

"I only said 'probably'," pointed out Elizabeth. "The usual doctor gave the usual death certificate. Of course, she may have committed suicide."

"Whyever would she have done that?" asked "Old Maree" in horror. "She was doing all right, wasn't she? I can't see what would have made her think of such a thing!"

"Boredom, perhaps," said Elizabeth. "But murder was a possibility, too. I didn't like the look of a character she was seeing a lot of at the end. Used to come up from the country somewhere to meet her. I'm country-bred myself. Father was MFH of the Pychesmore, as a matter of fact. This character did not look like a countryman to me."

"What did he look like?"

"Grey-haired, narrow face, weak expression. I should think he probably put weed-killer in her chocolates or something. She went out like a light. Up and about one week and faded altogether the next. Then they broke her door in and found her. The usual story."

"It's not the usual story!" said "Old Maree" indignantly. "Else I shouldn't be able to sleep at night for thinking of it. The way you talk, Elizabeth, is enough to turn anyone TT. You ought to be ashamed to talk like that!"

Elizabeth suppressed a yawn. "I only say what everyone else did at the time."

Once again, thought Carolus.

"Well, you shouldn't say it. I need something to pull me together after that. Yes, plain gin, please, and Elizabeth will have another brandy."

"I wasn't really sufficiently interested in the woman," went on Elizabeth in her bored voice. "She was terribly ordinary, really. Rather unusual in appearance, but there it stopped."

"In appearance?"

"She made me think of a giraffe. Not only the long neck but those large eyes, startled and longing, if you can see what I mean. She was put into cold storage till they could find her sister."

"Elizabeth!" said "Old Maree" rather hysterically. "I won't have it! What a way to speak! You give me the shudders. She means the mortuary," "Old Maree" added to Carolus.

"Yes," went on Elizabeth. "They raked up a married sister from somewhere who identified her and she was cremated. I ought to have gone to the cremation really, but I overslept."

"Old Maree" was calm again now and turned suitably philosophical. "Ah well," she said, "we all have to Go some time."

"Personally, I couldn't care less," said Elizabeth.

"Don't be so wicked. Of course you do. You've only got one life to live, you know. You're going to be a long time dead. So why not enjoy life while you can?"

"Enjoy it?" said Elizabeth contemptuously.

"Well, I do," said "Old Maree", "I know that. Always have done."

"You must be even more unintelligent than I thought."

"Who are you calling unintelligent?" asked "Old Maree", rhetorically. "At least I know what I want and how to get it which is more than some, however much they talk like someone on the BBC."

Carolus knew the high emotional pitch at which they lived and recognized this as a critical moment. Even Elizabeth with her blasé refinement was never far from hysteria. One sharp retort from her and there would be tears and violence. On the other hand a feather's weight would tip the whole crisis to laughter.

"I wish I did," he said. "I can't think what I want and if I could I shouldn't have a notion of how to get it. Except very simple things—like another drink. What about it?"

"This must be the last," said "Old Maree". "Plain gin and a nice brandy for Elizabeth."

An olive branch, perceived Carolus, and left them without misgivings while he went to the bar. All was well when he returned.

"Is there anything else you want to know about Frenchy?" asked Elizabeth. "Because I really must run after this."

"There was no real reason for thinking she was murdered, was there?" asked Carolus seriously.

"I suppose not, really. It was just what was said and that means very little."

"Or that she committed suicide?"

"That could be. I wouldn't like to give an answer on that. I didn't really know her well enough. And that's a dam' silly thing to say, too, because who the hell knows anyone well enough to anticipate their suicide?"

"I suppose not."

"Though I don't believe the old gag about people who threaten to do it not doing it. I've known too many who have threatened for years and then *have* done it."

"You never heard Frenchy threaten it?"

"I didn't. I didn't really know her."

"Cara would tell you that," put in "Old Maree". "If anyone had heard her it would have been Cara. You find her and you'll learn all you want."

"That may not be so easy. You don't remember her husband's first name, do you?"

"Morry, she called him."

"Maurice, then, or Morris, I suppose. I'll look it up later. I thank you both very much."

"Yes, but what about . . ." began "Old Maree" without budging.

Carolus, who had prepared for this while up at the bar, gave her his hand with the necessary Treasury Notes. She nodded, then said, "I dare say Elizabeth would . . ."

Carolus gave a laden hand to Elizabeth.

"I must be on my way," said "Old Maree". "This won't buy the baby a new frock." Not, perhaps, the happiest of phrases in the circumstances, thought Carolus. "I hope you find whoever it is you're looking for, and if you want to see me again I'm usually in here about nine."

Elizabeth nodded coolly and walked away.

11

It was time to see Mrs Chalk again. She had instigated the whole inquiry and should be kept informed, and there was a question which Carolus wanted to ask her. She was still staying with the Gorringers, and it was to their house that Carolus went at the headmaster's invitation to "take tea" as soon as he had returned to Newminster.

"We are all a-gog," said Mr Gorringer as he admitted Carolus, "and have little doubt that you will have fireworks for us, my dear Deene. We all have the greatest confidence in your ability to unravel this mystery."

He led the way to the drawing-room, normally kept for the reception of parents, but today warmed by a log fire and, in spite of a smell of damp upholstery being dried, rather inviting.

Mrs Gorringer quoted Robert Louis Stevenson: "'Home is the sailor, home from sea, And the hunter home from the hill.' Muswell or Campden, Mr Deene? Where has the chase taken you?"

Carolus was tired and rather nauseated by the case and found it hard to respond civilly to the facetiousnes of the Gorringers. He determined to let them see that this was very far from a humorous affair. He greeted Mrs Chalk, who looked as serious as he did.

"I have seen Rathbone," he said shortly.

"Ah *ha!*" cried Mr Gorringer. "I thought you would not let the grass grow under your feet. When and where did your meeting take place?"

"At about one o'clock in the morning in the cottage at Bluefield which he had once occupied."

"How did he account for the non-appearance of his wife?"

"He has to account for the non-appearance, as you put it, not of one woman but of three at least."

"You alarm me, Deene. Are you suggesting . . ."

"I'll tell you what I have discovered," said Carolus, and did so without circumlocution but in detail. He did not spare them the talk of murder in four places, Bluefield, Hastings, Bolderton and Montgolfier Street. He did not spare them the police search of Glose Cottage or the recollections of Miss Ramble. He gave them "Old Maree" and Elizabeth, full length, and the death of Frenchy exactly as he had heard it.

"What a sordid mare's nest you have disturbed, Deene!" said Mr Gorringer gravely. "You certainly have a *penchant* for the leprous and macabre. Who would have thought that a simple query like that of Mrs Chalk would have caused you to stir such muddy waters?"

"Perhaps you thought it would be a sort of jolly treasure hunt?" said Carolus rather bitterly.

"I did not think it would put you on the trail of a mass murderer," said Mr Gorringer, in his turn somewhat heated. "I still feel that only your morbid way of seeing these things is probably to blame. By your own account you have but the testimony of a few perhaps unreliable witnesses on which to base your assertion that there are three disappearances instead of one."

"You may be right," said Carolus wearily. Then turning to Mrs Chalk he asked, "Did you know your cousin Charlotte?"

"Scarcely at all," she said. "I don't suppose I saw her more than twice. We did not meet as children, and from the age of seventeen Charlotte was not considered by my parents as a suitable companion. I knew Anne much better than her unfortunate sister."

But Mr Gorringer returned to the attack.

"There is a point here which I am at a loss to understand. Since you suspect this man Rathbone of such a terrible series of brutal crimes, how did you allow him to slip through your fingers? There, by your own account, you had him. But you left him at large."

"What would you expect me to do? So far as I know there is no charge against him. Was I to hold him by force? It would make pretty headlines, *Kidnapping by Schoolmaster*, if that is what you wanted, Headmaster."

"Heaven forbid!" cried Mr Gorringer devoutly. "I see your difficulty. But could you not have wrung from him the truth about this strange affair?"

"I had no thumbscrews handy," said Carolus. "But I think you can put your mind at rest. When the police want him, they will be able to find him. They're very good at that sort of thing."

"Meanwhile, do you anticipate any further . . ."

"Murder? No."

There was a long silence of the kind which novelists used to designate "pregnant".

"And what will be your next steps?" asked Mr Gorringer at last.

"I'm going to the firm of wholesale chemists for which Rathbone used to work."

"Chemists?" said Mrs Gorringer. "I t'ink I smella da Rathbone."

"Poison, eh?" said her husband, comprehendingly.

"I want to see whether anyone there remembers him. It's fifteen years ago and that's quite a time."

"I cannot but feel, my dear Deene, that it is much to be regretted that we recommended you to Mrs Chalk. We were under a complete misapprehension. We supposed that we should be providing you with no more than a light holiday task. Now all my fears for the good name of the school are reawakened. Do you not feel that there is yet time for you to withdraw? After all, the police, as you say, have searched the cottage at Bluefield and must be hot on the scent. Can I not prevail upon you to spend the rest of your vacation in your comfortable home?"

"I couldn't do that, Headmaster," said Carolus gently.

"Of course he couldn't," put in Mrs Chalk. "He has to prove the thing, hasn't he? You are forgetting that my children cannot inherit their legacy until it is known beyond doubt that my cousin Anne is dead."

Mr Gorringer glanced at her reproachfully but said no more.

When Carolus reached his home it was time for the whisky and soda he enjoyed after a day's work and before his dinner. When Mrs Stick brought it, Carolus greeted her cheerfully.

"Tea at the headmaster's," he said.

"I expect you're tired then, sir. Would it be out of place for me to inquire whether that lady is still staying there?"

"Mrs Chalk? Yes. She's there."

The housekeeper showed by the taut expression on her face that she had guessed as much.

"I do hope you're going to have a few quiet days now," she said. "I was only saying to Stick, you need a rest if ever anyone did."

"I have to run up to town tomorrow, I'm afraid."

"Oh!" said Mrs Stick balefully.

He found that the premises of Tonkins Sons and Company in Hammersmith consisted of a warehouse and offices. At a very small pigeon-hole near the entrance he asked for Mr Tonkins.

"There is no Mr Tonkins now," said a voice from within.

"The manager, then," said Carolus.

"Which department?"

"Oh, hell, give me someone at the top who has been a long time with the firm!"

"That would be Mr Schmidt—well, Mr Villiers he is now since he became managing director instead of general manager as he'd always been. I don't know whether he can see you. What is your business?"

Carolus was tempted to say "Murder", and leave it at that.

"It's a confidential question connected with one of the staff."

A sniff came from the direction of the voice.

"That'll be just his tea, the nosy old so-and-so! I'll tell him."

After waiting a few minutes Carolus was taken up by lift and shown in to a small but showy room. It seemed that scarcely a firm with which this one did business had failed to send Mr Villiers some token engraved or printed indelibly with their name and business. Ash-trays, paperweights, ink-pots, calendars, paper-knives, framed prints, toys, ornaments, cigarette boxes were all tokens of regard if not affection from famous companies. A brand-new carpet and an outsize desk may have been installed to give prestige to the newly-named and recently created managing director.

"A confidential matter? You may speak in confidence," said Mr Villiers eagerly. He was a hawklike man who wore too many rings.

"I wanted to ask you about a man named Rathbone."

Mr Villiers pulled out a file.

"We have no such name on our books." he said.

"No. It is some years since you employed him."

"Really? How many years?

The interest of Mr Villiers did not seem to flag.

"About fifteen."

"Fifteen. Oh, Rathbone. You mean *Rathbone!*"

"Yes," said Carolus mildly.

"I remember Rathbone. I thought you meant someone we employed today," said Mr Villiers regretfully. "What about Rathbone?" His hopes seemed to rise again. "In some trouble?"

"He has disappeared. Also his wife."

"Good gracious! But why come to us? It is only by the merest chance that I remember the fellow. He was in my department or I should not have been able to tell you anything."

"I've come to you because I am trying to trace his life right back. Did he work here long?"

"I can turn up the record, but it was certainly for a considerable time. From a date before the outbreak of the war."

"Please don't bother," said Carolus politely, but Mr Villiers was proud of his files and not to be denied.

"Let's see. R. 1945 it would have been when he left us. Yes, he had been with us for fourteen years. Brigham Rathbone. Born 1908. I remember him well. Rather a shifty-looking man, I always thought. He surprised us by leaving to get married."

"Why did it surprise you?"

"He didn't seem the marrying type. He was less than forty at the time, I see, but I recollect him as looking nearer fifty."

"You did not know the lady he married?"

"Oh, yes I did," said Mr Villiers triumphantly. "A Miss Bright. She was the daughter of our chartered accountant. Her father, Herbert Bright, was the senior partner of a firm called Bright and Endive who had done our books for years. After his death we changed to our present accountants; but Herbert Bright was a friend of one of the Tonkins family and during his lifetime we should have gone to no one else."

"So that is how Rathbone met his wife?"

"In a way, yes. At that time the firm had an Amateur Dramatic Society which produced a play every winter, a record which was not broken even during the war years. Miss Bright used to take a part—not the principal part, which was taken by Miss Sylvia Tonkins, who was a most attractive young lady. But Miss Bright was keen. She would play perhaps the French maid or the secretary, or the elder sister: minor roles, but still essential to the play."

"And Rathbone?"

"He was something of a character actor and our expert on make-up. I remember old Mr Tonkins saying that it was the only time in the year when Rathbone came to life. He certainly didn't seem to have much enthusiasm for anything else."

"Was he a satisfactory employee?"

"Oh, he did his work or he wouldn't have stayed here, even during the war when we were very short-handed. Rathbone was unfit for war service, by the way. We have a very high standard. But he only just did his work, if you know what I mean. Never more than he needed. There was something rather supine about him. Old Mr Tonkins, who was very shrewd, called him lazy but never lazy enough to be in trouble. I don't know whether you have labor trouble but, if so, you'll know the type."

Carolus thought of his school class, the Lower Sixth, and nodded.

"So Rathbone became engaged to Miss Bright through the Amateur Dramatic Society?"

"Indirectly, yes. But not during Mr Bright's lifetime. There was a lot of trouble about it because they met about a year before Herbert Bright died, as he did quite suddenly of ptomaine poisoning, I believe. He was very upset about it. He was devoted to his daughter and not at all pleased when he found that she was receiving attention from Rathbone. Rathbone was ten years older than she was and looked more; he had no money of his own and very small prospects. Herbert Bright had always had big ideas for his daughter. She was, I can't help saying, rather a plain young woman, meager and not very healthy-looking. But her father adored her and complained bitterly to Mr Tonkins that an attachment had been allowed to begin and grow during the rehearsals for . . . let's see, *The Dover Road* was the play that year. Mr Tonkins was very upset about it, too, and the annual play was discontinued. However, when Herbert died and his daughter inherited, Rathbone lost no time at all. Within a year of the funeral the two were married and Rathbone gave up his position here, presumably to live on his wife's money."

"Did you find the attachment extraordinary?"

"For my own part, yes. But, strange as it may seem, this man Rathbone had an extraordinary attraction for a certain kind of woman. I even heard it described as mesmeric. He had rather strange eyes, with an expression hurt, watchful, timid, I scarcely know, yet seemingly able to achieve a quite hypnotic effect. The men here were surprised, but the women claimed to have foreseen it."

"I understand. You have a very good memory, Mr Villiers. May I try your patience a little further? There are several more questions I want to ask."

"By all means."

"First, where did Herbert Bright live?"

"Somewhere north of London. Watford, Bushey, Enfield, Potter's Bar, I forget exactly. I live in Surrey myself."

"Did Rathbone go to his home?"

"During his lifetime? I should think almost certainly not. Herbert Bright couldn't bear him."

"And—this is probably asking too much—where did Rathbone live?"

"I can tell you exactly," said Mr Villiers. "Not very far from here. At a private hotel, as it called itself, at Barnes. The Athlone, or was it the Connaught? No, the Lascelles. Here it is: the Lascelles Private Hotel, St Andrew's Avenue. It was in reality a boarding-house with pretensions. Rathbone lived there for many years, I believe."

"You knew it?"

"On one occasion I found it necessary to call on Rathbone. I was not then a director of this firm, you understand. Yes, I saw the place. Rathbone could go almost from door to door by bus."

"And after the time of his marriage you saw no more of him?"

"No. I seem to remember hearing that he was living at Bolderton, but that is all."

"Now here is something which I want to ask you, Mr Villiers, which you may not feel inclined to answer. I know very little of your business, but I take it that like other wholesale chemists you handle what are called dangerous drugs?"

"We do, of course."

"And without going into toxicological details there are many that are poisonous?"

"In certain conditions, yes."

"Had Rathbone access to such?"

"Access, perhaps. But access is one thing, the facility to abstract is another. We flatter ourselves on a checking system which is impregnable. No irregularity was reported during the whole of Rathbone's time with us. Handling chemicals as we do, we have learned to take the most scrupulous care."

"Still, again speaking as a layman, I should have thought it impossible to be absolutely certain."

"If you are interested, I will show you our system."

"No. It's very kind of you, but I will certainly accept your word."

"I could not, of course, go into Court and say under oath that it would be impossible for an employee to remove sufficient of one chemical or another to cause death. I can only say that our system makes it extremely unlikely. Things which would be on the poison list of any retail chemist are kept with special safeguards and Rathbone would have had no means of defeating these. But do you suspect him of having done so?"

"I think you will find that the police will, Mr Villiers. I should be surprised if you are not asked to explain that system of yours to someone with more technical knowledge than mine. Someone who, perhaps, might be able to pick holes in it."

"That I very much doubt."

"I am most grateful to you for all your help and information. It is most unusual to obtain such lucid details of events fifteen years ago."

"In matters that affect our staff here, I believe my memory is reliable. In a large firm like this there are always problems and I make it my business to know as much as possible of our employees. It would take a clever man or woman to escape my eye in anything that might be deleterious to the firm."

"I'm sure it would."

"And what I see, I remember. I am glad to have been of assistance to you."

As Carolus was about to leave the building, the disembodied voice from the pigeon-hole asked: "Get what you wanted?"

"Yes, thanks."

"I thought you would. There's nothing he doesn't know. Talk about snooping!"

"Really?"

"Chronic," said the voice. "Ta-ta, then."

Carolus wondered whether "Be seeing you" would be a suitable form of leave-taking, but in the circumstances decided against it.

12

This was all very well, thought Carolus as he drove the short distance to Barnes, but where was it going to stop? It was useful to find Rathbone so clearly remembered by people as different as Miss Ramble and Villiers but each of them sent him farther back into Rathbone's past till at last, if he was not careful, he would find himself hearing details of childhood and parents or even become embroiled in the complications of heredity.

Yet how could he neglect the Lascelles Private Hotel? Doubtless there would be a garrulous proprietress who would be set on giving him recollections of Rathbone's diet and table manners, but there might be something far more relevant, as there had been among the oddments remembered by Mr Villiers. And secretly he had a faint hope, based on little more than guesswork and intuition, that he might hear something more recent about Rathbone. At all events he could not afford to pass over the place, though he was determined to regard it as the last outpost on the road to the past. If he was told about the family home from which

Rathbone had moved to the Lascelles Private Hotel as a young man he would ignore it.

He found it, in the words of Villiers, "a boarding-house with pretensions". The pretensions consisted, on the outside, of large gilt lettering running across the face of the house next door as well (doubtless by arrangement with its owner) and gilt tops to the iron railings. In a small room labelled "Residents' Lounge" he faced the proprietress.

"Oh but we've only been here about a year," she said, faintly amused at his question. "You're going back into history. The people before us didn't have it more than three years, I believe, so goodness knows who was here fifteen years ago."

"I could not expect my luck to continue forever," smiled Carolus, rising. "I've been very fortunate so far in tracing the man I want."

"Sorry I can't help you, but we're not quite ante-diluvian, you know."

As Carolus was leaving, the proprietress remembered something. "Now I come to think of it, I believe there *is* a chance," she said. "We've got an old Colonel here now. He's only been with us a week or so, but he came because he had stayed here, he said, in the old days. Colonel Hood. You could ask him if you like."

"Is he in?"

"Not at the minute. But he'll be in before lunch, which is at one-thirty. They never miss meals," added the proprietress with a touch of asperity. "As a matter of fact he's the only one who has lunch here at the moment. All the rest are bed and breakfast people who go to work."

"It's twenty to one now."

"Then he won't be long. You may depend on that. Why don't you sit down and wait?"

"It's very kind of you."

The proprietress was right. Not ten minutes later a jaunty figure in an Anthony Eden hat passed the window and entered. Carolus heard him greeted.

"Oh there you are, Colonel Hood. There's a gentleman in the lounge waiting to see you."

A cheerful voice said, "Thank you, Mrs D," and the Colonel entered.

Carolus recognized him at once. The sharp white military moustache, the monocle cord, the striped tie which would have delighted Mr Lofting, the neat dark clothes and the padded chest did not disguise the person of Rathbone.

Carolus could not resist a touch of old melodrama.

"So we meet again," he said.

Rathbone quickly shut the door behind him and did what "Old Maree" was determined not to do—crumpled.

"How did you find me?" he said brokenly.

"I told you it would be easy when the time came."

Carolus was pleased that his luck was running, after all. It had occurred to him as a remote possibility that Rathbone, whose knowledge of other cities could not be extensive, would probably be in London and might conceivably have gravitated to the place in which he had previously lived. But that "Colonel Hood" would be Rathbone himself had never entered his mind.

"They say that murderers return to the scenes of their crimes," went on Carolus, "so perhaps widowers return to the scenes of their bachelordom. You *are* a widower, aren't you, Rathbone?"

"What right have you to ask me?"

"None. But I'm very curious. I'm going to ask you quite a lot before I leave. If I do leave without you."

Rathbone stood up shakily.

"You're not a policeman," he said.

"No. But that can very easily be remedied if you prefer talking to the police. I told you they would search Glose Cottage."

A hint of triumph was in Rathbone's voice as he turned on Carolus.

"And what did they find?" he asked defiantly.

Carolus watched him.

"A pair of ear-rings," he said quietly.

Rathbone crumpled again.

"They also looked for fingerprints," said Carolus.

"And didn't find any!"

"That's the point. Like the dog that barked in the night. There were no fingerprints."

Rathbone sat looking at the floor. Presently he said—"Are they looking for me?"

"I don't know. I'm not in their confidence. They hadn't been to Hastings when I was there."

A sound like a groan came from Rathbone. "Hastings?" he repeated.

"Miss Ramble is still there. She has the liveliest of recollections of your stay there with the lady whom I must describe as your second wife. Nor, I think, have the police interviewed 'Old Maree'." Watching Rathbone, Carolus thought this name had entirely misfired. "About Frenchy, I mean, and Cara." That went home all right.

"You . . . you . . ."

"I haven't wasted my time looking for you, Rathbone. I've gone back, not forward. Back to Coleshill Lodge." That really struck.

"I didn't kill her," Rathbone murmured suddenly.

"Whom didn't you kill?"

"Anyone. I didn't kill anyone. Oh, God!"

Was the man going to faint again?

"Relax," said Carolus. "Why don't you go and get it all off your chest? You needn't tell me anything. But the police will soon know all I do, and more. I can't see what good you do yourself by trying to live under a disguise."

There was no answer.

"You know the police dug up every possible patch of ground at Glose Cottage. They'll do the same at Coleshill Lodge when they get on to it."

This was the most critical moment in the interview and at first Carolus thought the careful words had been ineffective. But no. The face which Rathbone turned up to him had an expression of sheer agony and the man had a paroxysm of trembling.

"So why not get it over?" ended Carolus.

Still no reply.

"You see, Rathbone, you are dealing with a very determined woman in Mrs Chalk. In order to obtain their inheritance for her children, she won't hesitate to let you hang."

The moustache, so slick and jaunty a few minutes ago, seemed to have sagged with Rathbone's whole body. It was hard not to feel some pity for the man.

"Why did you give up your job with Tonkins when you married?" asked Carolus more casually.

"I hated it."

"The firm, you mean?"

"No the work. I have always hated work." Carolus realized that he was hearing the cardinal fact about this man. It was almost Rathbone's religion. "I never meant to do another day's work in my life. And I sha'n't."

Interesting, that. It had put real animation into Rathbone for a moment.

"When did you first see your wife's sister Charlotte?"

"When Annie was ill at Bolderton. She came down. Annie had kept in touch with her, secretly of course. If her father had known, he would have been furious. Annie asked me to send for her."

"And when did you see her last?"

Rathbone thought carefully.

"Alive, never," he said. "We saw her in the mortuary."

"So far as you could tell in death, was she much changed? It was four years after her visit to Bolderton."

Rathbone seemed puzzled by this question, or perhaps he was trying to guess Carolus's reason for asking it.

"No," he replied. "So far as one could tell, very little."

Carolus nodded.

"You never met her friend Cara then?"

"Cara? No. We met none of her associates."

"How do you account for the fact that everyone at Bolderton remembers your wife as being small and almost emaciated, everyone at Hastings as heavy and round-cheeked, everyone at Bluefield as tall, perpetually smiling and elderly?"

The answer when it came was so absurd that Carolus had to suppress a smile. Yet it seemed to him in the circumstances the only possible answer.

"People change," said Rathbone.

"Their height—in middle age?"

"Shoes," said Rathbone. "High heels."

It was the turn of Carolus to say nothing. When he spoke, it was on quite another matter.

"Why were you so upset when Mrs Luggett heard you'd lived at Hastings? Since you had nothing to hide, as you say, why should that have worried you?"

Rathbone muttered something about other people minding their own business. Then said bitterly to Carolus: "You must have been busy. All these details!"

"I have," said Carolus. "But I haven't finished yet. I'm going to get the whole story from the beginning to . . . to the very unpleasant end. I know a good deal more than when we met before, but still not enough. I notice, for instance, that you have had your teeth attended to. Was that part of your make-up as Colonel Hood?"

"I suppose so."

"But why bother with all this, Rathbone? You must have known you would be found quickly enough when the time came."

"How did you find me?" asked Rathbone sombrely.

"Schmidt is still at Tonkins. His name is Villiers now that he's a director. He knew where you lived when you worked there."

"But I don't see how you could guess I should return. It's uncanny."

"Are you a Christian Scientist?" asked Carolus suddenly.

"I? No. Why?"

"You were at Hastings."

"A fad of my wife's. Soon disappeared."

"As she did."

"For a time, yes."

"Somehow Christian Science and Church at Bluefield don't fit very well. Nor does the song over which you quarrelled with Miss Ramble."

"That was ridiculous. There was nothing in the song. She was a narrow-minded woman."

"Yes. I dare say. But your wife's character seems to have changed almost as often as her height and weight. The only thing that remained unchanged was her signature. But I suppose that was the main thing."

"You're wrong," said Rathbone. "I was very fond of Annie."

"But you hated work?"

"Yes."

"There were other inconsistencies, you know. At Bolderton your wife was so abstemious that she had the greatest difficulty in swallowing a little milk-stout when the doctor ordered it for her. At Hastings she drank 'more than was good for her' and went often to the Star and Mitre. At Bluefield she was TT again. How come?"

"Sea air," said Rathbone gloomily.

"Sea air my foot! Then there was her health. At Bolderton she was suffering from pernicious anaemia and was regarded as a chronic invalid. At Hastings she was rubicund and cheerful and at Bluefield she never had a day's illness. How do you think you're going to explain all this to the police? They're not complete nit-wits, you know. People's memories are long. Admittedly at Hastings you lived between two ferocious old gossip-mongers, Miss Ramble and Mrs Bishop. But Mrs Richards who worked for you at Bolderton is no fool and does not exaggerate 'nor set down aught in malice'. Then Villiers, ex-Schmidt, delights in remembering everything for the sake of it. So does Potter, the clerk in Mumford's office. You were too recently at Bluefield to be out of anyone's recollection. How *do* you think you're going to get away with it?"

Rathbone made silence and resignation his refuge. Then Carolus fired a question at him of a different, a far more direct kind while he watched his face.

"Did you know Montgolfier Street?" he asked.

Rathbone took his time.

"I've heard of it," he said.

"You have never been there?"

"Not to my knowledge. Where is it?"

Carolus did not answer.

"You tell me you never met your wife's sister except when she came down to Bolderton, so you didn't know a woman known as 'Old Maree'?"

"Certainly not."

"Nor one called 'Elizabeth'?"

"No."

"Nor a man known as 'Daddy' Makroides?"

"I've never heard the name."

Here, Carolus felt, he was wasting time. Unless he was very much mistaken, Rathbone was speaking the truth. But Carolus tried again.

"What was the cause of Frenchy's death?"

"Frenchy?" said Rathbone warily.

"Your sister-in-law."

"Oh, yes. I was forgetting she used another name. I don't think I ever knew how she died. Undernourishment had something to do with it, I should say."

"You don't think she committed suicide?"

"I've no means of knowing. A doctor gave a certificate. If I ever knew, I forget now what he gave as the cause."

"Were you aware that there was talk of murder?"

"I wasn't; but I imagine it wouldn't be unusual in a case like that."

Rathbone seemed strangely unruffled by this. But he could not conceal a start when Carolus followed up these questions with another.

"Do you know a Mrs Myberg?" he asked.

Not for at least twenty seconds did he say: "No." Then it was in a low voice. But he rallied to fire back: "Who is she?"

"She used to be known as Cara."

"I know nothing about her. Nothing."

"You don't even know that she lives in Bayswater?"

"No."

Carolus had nearly finished. He tried one more question.

"I gather you are an expert in make-up?"

Surely, Carolus thought, Rathbone could throw that away lightly? No. His face remained grave.

"Where did you hear that? Oh, at Tonkins's, I suppose. I was interested in amateur theatricals. That's all."

"Hence Colonel Hood, I suppose?"

"I have explained that." Then Rathbone asked flatly the question which must have been most in his mind—perhaps for years.

"What is going to happen?"

"Your guess is as good as mine. But I have warned you that Coleshill Lodge will almost certainly be searched as thoroughly as Glose Cottage was. And the garden. I imagine that the answer to your question depends very largely on what is found there. Personally, I'm going back to Bluefield this afternoon."

Just then a gong was beaten. Carolus rose.

"Your lunch," he said, watching Rathbone.

For a long time the man did not move. Then he stood up, squared his shoulders in a pitiful attempt to resume the character of Colonel Hood, and marched out of the room.

Carolus was about to leave when the proprietress returned. "Did you find out what you wanted?" she asked brightly.

"Not everything," said Carolus, "but quite a lot."

"Colonel Hood did remember your man, then?"

"Yes. He remembered him well."

"*Isn't* Colonel Hood a nice old gentleman? Quite my favorite among the guests. One of the old school. So kind and gentle. Wouldn't hurt a fly."

"A fly?" said Carolus absently. "No. I'm sure he wouldn't."

"And do you know—I can't help smiling—he has a lady friend! Yes, really. She comes to see him now and again. I always leave them the lounge."

"Really?" said Carolus as though enjoying the sentimental humor of it. "What is she like?"

"She's not young. Very cheerful and pleasant. Nothing extra-ordinary about her. Wears rather too much jewellery, perhaps. They sit and chat. It's rather touching."

"Would you describe her as a powerful-looking woman?"

"You *do* ask some questions! She's not an Amazon, exactly, but I shouldn't like to fall out with her, if you know what I mean. I should think she could give as good as she got. She wanted an armchair nearer the fire one day and just picked it up as though it were nothing. Now I must go and see to the lunch."

Carolus took his departure and drove away; but he did not take the route by which he had come. He turned north through Willesden and Wembley. After an uninteresting lunch at the snack bar of a roadside pub, he continued his way towards Bolderton. He was taking a chance. At least he might make an almighty fool of himself; at the worst he might be causing serious trouble, even danger. But he was doing what he had done from the beginning of this case, believing that in this way alone he would find the answer. *He was putting himself in Rathbone's place.*

13

HE could at first think of no way in which to pass the next four hours in these bright built-up areas of innumerable new houses. In spite of the very real urgency of the situation, he did not want to call at Coleshill Lodge till nearly seven o'clock, when Humbell would have finished the evening meal which he ate on his return from the office. It was a stark and weary prospect, for the time now was a quarter to three and round him stretched the endless monotones of an afternoon in new suburbs. He wanted to sit and think as he could at Newminster in the warmth of his own pleasant sitting-room. Then suddenly he remembered the cinema. He drove on till he found a cinema showing an American film which could not conceivably distract him from his thoughts, and entered. It was warm and nearly empty.

As for thinking, he soon passed into a snoozy reverie in which the case he was investigating was no more real than the figures on the screen. Three disappearances and—was there a death connected with the thing? He remembered Elizabeth's matter-of-fact what-do-you-expect attitude about "Frenchy". The usual doctor gave the usual certificate, she said, after blowing out with her cigarette smoke the suggestion "probably murdered". Then there was the fact—surely irrelevant but still in the circumstances noteworthy—that Herbert Bright had died at an extremely convenient moment of ptomaine poisoning as Villiers called it, probably using an out-moded term for botulism.

In any case three disappearances. Only in the first had Rathbone not said plaintively to some one, "my wife has left me". The "first Mrs Rathbone", as Carolus for the sake of convenience called Anne, had not apparently "left" him as the other two, if there were two others, had done. Either she had gone with him from Coleshill Lodge or . . . been left behind. At all events no one, to the knowledge of Carolus, had set eyes on any person answering to her description since Mrs Richards and Dr Whistley, who had seen her weak and ill in her room at Coleshill Lodge. Unless, of course, thought Carolus dreamily, either Christian Science or Hastings air was so miraculous in its effect that within a few weeks of taking to them Anne had become a buxom woman who liked a drink and sang vulgar songs at the piano.

Then there was the second disappearance from Hastings, this time with suitcases in the car, and Rathbone's return late at night and subsequent wailings that he had been deserted. If the "second Mrs Rathbone" was not Anne, whence had she risen and to what cheerful haven had she afterwards retired? Terrestrial or not? She had been a friendly soul and had identified the body of "Frenchy". That seemed to argue that she and Anne were one. "People change" said Rathbone. Could he be so far right?

As for the "third Mrs Rathbone" with her toothy grin and reluctance to chatter—what a change was here! If a woman could change to that extent, so abruptly and so much for the worse, it was a nightmare world. Yet she had been recognized by Mumford's clerk Potter as the original inheritor of Herbert Bright's estate who had also called at the office during her residence at Hastings. Very confusing, that. It really began to look as though Mr Mumford was right when he said he had heard too many descriptions in Court to take any notice of them.

There was an explanation, of course, and one which covered every inconsistency, but it was of a nature so macabre that Carolus did not want to accept it. Yet, was anything too macabre for belief? Three seeming disappearances, two possible murders—what were these to the seventy-odd which Petiot claimed or even for the thirty for which he was guillotined?

At all events tonight should decide. Unless he was wrong in his basic plan of campaign, which consisted in putting himself in Rathbone's place, tonight should yield the information he needed. Not a complete explanation; but at least all that was necessary at this time. There might still be some spadework to be done. (He smiled unhappily over the term.) But most of that could be left to the police.

Reaching Bolderton at last, Carolus regretfully garaged his car. He might need it urgently, but the risk of it standing, so easily recognizable, in the street was too great. He went on foot to Coleshill Lodge. Humbell himself opened the door.

"I'm awfully sorry to trouble you again," began Carolus.

"Oh, yes. You came to make inquiries about the Rathbones. Do come in."

He was shown into the sitting-room in which he had interviewed the Humbells during his previous call; it looked very cosy, with warmly shaded lights and a good fire. Mrs Humbell put down her book and he saw that by the other armchair were the evening paper, Humbell's pipe and a tumbler.

"Have a drink?" said Humbell. "I've got some whisky, if you like that, or a bottle of beer."

"Before you are so hospitable, you had better hear what I've come about," said Carolus smiling.

"Nonsense. Give me your coat. Whisky, I'm sure."

It occurred to Carolus that although these people were contented, happy to be together in the home they had made cheerful, they welcomed the diversion of his visit. They had their share of curiosity and in the years they had lived here had probably speculated often about their mysterious predecessors. They were very English, perhaps what is rather fatuously called commonplace people. The man would be considered sound, reliable, straight as a die, competent and no fool. The wife was sensible, kindly, shrewd and calm.

"It's strange you should bring up all this about the Rathbones," said Humbell when they were at ease. "We often used to wonder about them when we first came. There was a lot of foolish talk at the time. But we had only recently lost our only son in the war and wanted to move nearer London. We were delighted to find this place, which was just the right size when there were only the two of us. So we weren't going to be put off by gossip about it, were we, dear?"

Mrs Humbell smiled. "We even heard it was haunted," she said.

"Yes. But we're the wrong people for that sort of nonsense. We've never seen or heard anything out of the way since we came here."

"That, I'm afraid, is what I've come to tell you. I think you may see or hear something tonight."

Humbell grinned. "A ghost?" he asked.

"No. But a visitor. Look, Mr Humbell, I'm going to risk your thinking me a bore or a bringer of bad luck or whatnot. I'm going to tell you exactly what I believe and leave it to you to act as you think best. But before I do so, I must say that I may be hopelessly wrong. I haven't a scrap of proof to go on. I'm trusting entirely to two things, my instincts and the experience I have accumulated in working out a number of rather curious cases.

"Also I want to say how sorry I am that you two should be dragged into something so unpleasant. But it just can't be helped. If I am right, when you took this house you inherited with it not only the excellent Mrs Richards but the Rathbone mystery. And a mystery it still is."

Humbell pulled at his pipe. "I expect we can take it," he said. "Would you explain a little more clearly?"

"Of course. There is reason to think that the woman Rathbone married, with whom he lived here for about eight years, is either missing or dead. I am convinced that somewhere in this house, or more probably in the garden, is concealed some kind of evidence which will enable us to trace her, whether she is alive or dead."

"What makes you think that?"

"I have told you it is little more than an instinct. If she is alive, there is still something here which troubles Rathbone. But more probably she is dead."

"You mean, to be frank, that you think her remains are here?"

"You use the very word, though I did not like to put it in that way. Remains are all that can possibly exist, and there may be very little of them. Fourteen years is a long time. But something is here, I feel sure. You must have heard from Mrs Richards how the house was left. First they dismissed the nurse. Then, for no reason at all that she could see, Mrs Richards herself. Then, on the day before the doctor was due to pay his weekly visit, *but two or three days after Mrs Richards had left*, the house was vacated after dark. No one saw them go. There were no houses adjoining this then, and no one heard them. When the doctor arrived next day there was no one here."

"Yes. It's odd. We've often thought so."

"But what makes it so much more odd, Mr Humbell, is that much the same thing has happened again. Not once, but twice. Rathbone went from here to Hastings and from there took his wife for a drive from which she never returned. From there he moved to a lonely village called Bluefield where he did the same. Meanwhile his sister-in-law in London died suddenly. And I find today that Rathbone is associating with a woman who calls at his boarding-house to confer with him. One begins to wonder where it will stop."

"I should think so. What are the police doing about it?"

"The police, to be fair, have not been given the facts of the case as I have. All they have been told, so far as I know, is that a man and his wife disappeared suddenly from a cottage at Bluefield."

"Oughtn't they to be told more?"

"As soon as there is anything to tell them. I don't think they'd be much interested in the kind of half-baked theorizing I've been doing this evening."

"One thing I'd like to know," said Mrs Humbell in her pleasant quiet voice, "is why you say 'tonight'? You said you thought something was going to happen tonight. Why?"

"Because," said Carolus slowly, "Rathbone learned today that the police associate him with this place and intend to search it as they searched the other cottage. If I am right in thinking that some evidence is concealed here, and if it is accessible, I don't think a moment will be wasted."

"It's a nice prospect," said Mr Humbell. "As I see it, you've practically come to warn us that we can expect a call from a murderer, perhaps a multiple murderer, in our home tonight."

"I haven't said quite that. But of course it's beastly. I have hated telling you about it."

"What do you suggest we should do?"

"I suggest you should let me stay down here by the fire. There is, thank heavens, a bright moon tonight and I can see most of the garden from this window. I know it's fearful presumption to suggest it, but it is not a case for beating about the bush."

Humbell exchanged glances with his wife. "You're welcome to stay so far as we're concerned," he said. "In fact we should be glad to have you in the house."

"You're showing great confidence in me. After all, you know nothing about me. I might be a mild lunatic with a bee in his bonnet about the Rathbones."

"I think I'm a pretty good judge of a man, Mr Deene," said Humbell, then added irrelevantly, or perhaps not quite irrelevantly: "Our son would have been just about your age, if he had lived. My wife even thinks there's a likeness. Anyhow, let's get down to brass tacks. You want to stay in this room because you think Rathbone will try to recover something he left behind. Is that it?"

"Rathbone or someone else, yes."

"Someone else? You did not say anything about that."

"This is a very strange affair, Mr Humbell. I do not know who may be involved. And I'm afraid I cannot be sure that, even if this happens, it will be tonight. It might be tomorrow or just possibly the next night, though I don't think so."

"I see. I'm out to help you in any way I can, but I still can't see why we don't simply call the police."

"There are several good reasons. They would not take seriously my idea of a visit tonight, for one. And they might scare our bird off, for another."

"Yes, I can see that."

"Now could you give me an idea about the garden? How it's laid out, I mean, and how anyone could enter it?"

"It's very easy to enter, as you must have seen. Down the road-side of it there are only the old park railings of the iron-hurdle type which a child can climb with a few shrubs behind them. Then most of it's a lawn, which was down when I came, with a perennial border round it."

"You've made very few changes?"

"Beyond building a wooden summer-house in the far corner, very few. In fact the plan is identical. All I have done is to grow things where there was nothing but weeds when I came. Rathbone can't have been much of a gardener."

"No. I've had cause to see that in his cottage at Bluefield. Where do you keep your gardening tools?"

"In the outside lavatory, which locks up. I take it that, if anything happens in the night, you'll call me?"

"I shall do nothing of the sort," smiled Carolus. "I don't expect to do more than observe, myself."

"But you won't let any evidence be taken away. There might be more than one intruder . . ." It was plain that Mr Humbell did not want to be left out of it.

"If I need any help," promised Carolus, "I'll give you a shout."

The two men had a last nightcap after Mrs Humbell had climbed the narrow stairs to her room. "It wouldn't be an easy house to break into, this," said Humbell. "All these diamond-paned windows have heavy metal frames."

"They wouldn't present much difficulty to an expert," said Carolus, "but an amateur would find them hard to manipulate silently. So far as we know, no one connected with this case is a professional screwsman. That is why I don't think whatever it is that's wanted can be in the house. I mean, if anyone comes at all he will come for something he knows he can get fairly easily; therefore my guess is that it's outside. I don't suppose you've had to go deeper than ordinary digging of the border?"

"No. Except when we built the summer-house. That has brick foundations. Just its four corners, I mean, to raise the wooden floor a few inches from the ground."

"There's no cellar under the house?"

"No."

"You have main drainage?"

"Yes. Well, Deene, help yourself to another whisky when you want it. You've got blankets there and quite a comfortable settee . . ."

"I shan't sleep."

"I'll wish you an interesting vigil then. I hope you'll have some breakfast with us tomorrow. It's Sunday and we usually take it pretty easy, but the wife will be down by about nine. Good night."

Carolus waited until Humbell had climbed the stairs, then turned out all lights in the room. The fire was burning low by then. He crossed to the windows and slowly drew back the long curtains. There was enough moonlight to see as far as the end of the little square of garden, but only to see a shadowy confusion of black and grey.

Carolus drew a chair to the window, choosing a straight-backed and none too comfortable one for fear of sleeping. He threw away his cigarette, whose little ember would be a signal to anyone in the garden. He picked up the blankets which Mrs Humbell had left him and drew them round him, meaning to let the fire go out. Even if anyone came close to the window and peered in now, Carolus would remain invisible. It would be a wretchedly uncomfortable vigil, and not for the first time he told himself he was a fool to have disturbed this friendly household and given himself a miserable night with so little to go on. But there came back to him the agonized look on Rathbone's face when Carolus had said that the police would search Coleshill Lodge. This recollection reassured him. He could not be wrong about tonight. What would Rathbone wait for? He had no reason to suspect as untrue Carolus's remark that he was going back to Bluefield today.

Rathbone, after all, was not, as Mrs Richards had said, at all handy about the house. There was little possibility of his having done a Dr Crippen; Mrs Richards was only out of the place for a week or so between her dismissal by Rathbone and her starting with the Humbells. If the flooring had been disturbed, she would have noticed it. The more Carolus considered, the more he was sure that the garden was the place, the logical, the only place. And tonight was the logical, the only time. He stared into the silver and jet of the little garden.

For two hours he remained there, growing stiff and cold. A pity, he thought, that Rathbone was not experienced in such nightwork; he would have known better than to leave it to the small hours when even his car might be noticed and he himself questioned on his way to or from Coleshill Lodge. Breaking and entering is mostly done before midnight, when a lorry rouses no question and men moving in the streets are less rare.

At something past one there was movement. The night was very still and the shrubs beside the iron fence were not moved by any passing breeze, but in one place only. He could not see any outlines, but presently a shadow emerged from the shadows and started to cross towards the summer-house. Then it stopped. It remained motionless for rather more than thirty seconds, then turned back towards the shrubbery. Carolus sprang to the light switch but, before the brilliant lights shone from the window across the little lawn, the shadow had time to return to the bushes by the rails; but not time quite to disappear. Carolus perceived only one thing before it dived into the blackness. It was a woman.

14

CAROLUS opened the window and jumped lightly out. But he knew he would not be in time, nor was he greatly concerned. He had not seen enough to recognize the figure, but he was pretty sure of its identity. He went to the point in the shrubbery through which the woman had disappeared and, pushing his way between damp branches, reached the railings. The little street was not well lit, but well enough for him to see that no one was in sight. As he stood there hesitating, he heard an engine started up and a car driven away. That was all right. He had learned what he expected but hated to learn.

Then he walked exactly as the woman must have done on entering the garden, as the shadow had moved, from the shrubbery across the lawn. Carolus stopped at the point where the shadow had stopped. As he had guessed, it was from here that the structure of the summer-house became apparent. It looked solid in the moonlight, like an old loggia. When he returned towards the house he saw that Humbell was at the window from which he had jumped.

"I'll open the garden door for you," said Humbell, but Carolus entered as he had come.

"What was it?" asked Humbell.

"Our visitor," said Carolus.

"Gone?"

"Yes. Gone. Not to return. Never to return, I am quite sure. Mr Humbell, what was in that corner of the garden before you built the summer-house there?"

"Nothing but a rubbish-heap. Why?"

"I think that's our spot."

"Under it, you mean?"

"Yes."

"That's awkward. It's too heavy to be lifted whole, even if we brought in a team to do it. Perhaps we can get the floorboards up."

"I'm afraid I've brought you nothing but trouble, Mr Humbell."

"Oh, I don't know. It would have come anyway, wouldn't it? The police would have got on to this before long. And I'm interested."

"You're very long-suffering. I'm afraid Mrs Humbell must be put out."

Humbell smiled. "My wife is *never* put out," he said proudly.

"Lucky man! Do you know it's nearly two o'clock?"

"Yes. We must get some sleep. You'll be all right on the settee?"

"Yes, thanks."

After a bath next morning and a cheerful breakfast with his hosts, Carolus could view his problem with more detachment.

"I've been thinking," said Humbell. "Mrs Richards's son-in-law is a carpenter. We might walk round there after breakfast and see whether he would like to tackle those floorboards."

"The only thing I insist on," said Carolus, "is that all expenses in the matter should be mine."

"I don't see why," said Humbell. "That floor is a bit rotten, I dare say, and I should have had to replace it some time. However, we'll discuss that when we know more."

Mrs Richards's son-in-law, a stalwart man who appeared to think deeply over his work, gave much the same opinion. "It wouldn't be worth replacing these," he said. "Nor the joists. They're too far gone. We could soon have them up and, if you like to get the material, I'll replace them next week-end."

So the earth under the summer-house was laid bare. "Who is going to turn the first sod?" asked Humbell when he had brought a spade. He did not wait for an answer, but began to dig in a steady professional sort of way, throwing the earth out on the lawn as he did so. Carolus raked this through as it fell. Then Mrs Richards's son-in-law took a turn with the spade and afterwards Carolus. But there was no need to search carefully through the upturned earth. Their discovery, when it came, was a gruesome one which needed no sifting of the ground. It was a human skull.

Mrs Richards's son-in-law stood staring down at it as Hamlet stared at another skull. Humbell said, "Good God!" and looked as though he were going to be sick. To Carolus it occurred that he had never seen an example of this so often depicted thing, and he fervently hoped that he would never do so again. It was grotesque beyond all imagining. Skull and cross-bones, skull in plaster labelled *memento mori*, skulls in pictures were clean and polished things of ivory. This was like an old bone long buried by a dog, rotten and muddy and horrifying. "That skull had a tongue in it, and could sing once" remembered Carolus, his imagination half with the grave-digger at Elsinore.

"Don't let the wife see it," said Humbell, pulling himself together. "Wait while I get a sack."

"We'll let the police do any more digging they want," said Carolus, when that vacantly grinning thing was out of sight. "It must of course be reported to them straight away. Will you phone, Mr Humbell? I have something urgent to do."

"Yes. I'll phone." He spoke firmly and was quite himself again. "I'll have to tell my wife first."

Carolus waited only to grab his coat and say that he would return later. He then hurried round to the garage in which he had left his car. Within ten minutes of their discovery he was travelling at an illegal speed towards Barnes. He had remembered that there was a telephone booth at the corner of St Andrew's Avenue and, leaving his car in a side-turning, he made for this. He dialled the number of the Lascelles Private Hotel and recognized the voice of the proprietress.

"Could I speak to Colonel Hood?" he asked.

"Well, you're just in time, because he has this minute phoned for a taxi. He's in a hurry but I'll call him."

Carolus put down the receiver while she was doing this and waited in the booth from which he could see the entrance to the Lascelles Private Hotel. In a few minutes the taxi came and Rathbone emerged carrying a suitcase. This was a tricky moment. Carolus could not go to his car till he saw which way the taxi went, but he knew he might lose it while he was starting and perhaps turning. He was lucky in that the taxi was an old one with, it seemed, an unhurried driver, and he easily found it again in the long road running towards Hammersmith. From there he followed it, though with more difficulty. It was going, he imagined, to one of the big railway stations, but it was not until it began to cross Waterloo Bridge that he could be certain which one. At that point he took a chance and, passing it, had time to park his car before it arrived.

He did not think himself particularly clever in this piece of deduction. A suitcase and a taxi meant one of two things—a London station or a London address. The chances were about seventy per cent in favor of a station, and they became ninety per cent on Waterloo Bridge. Rathbone was not brilliant, but he was not fool enough to leave a direct trail, which the taximan could describe afterwards, from his old address to a new one. Anyhow it worked. With a hastily-purchased copy of the *Observer* as cover, he watched Rathbone, a very unmilitary-looking Colonel Hood, make for the window of the booking-office from which tickets to the West Country were obtained. Carolus dared not follow closely enough to hear the name of the station for which Rathbone booked, but he noted that the man had no hesitation in asking for it. He had evidently planned this departure.

Carolus bought a single to Land's End, and was relieved to see that Rathbone called a porter for his bag. There was a brief conversation between Rathbone and the porter, after which Rathbone walked over to the buffet and Carolus could ask the porter, after tipping him, which train his client was taking. It was the three-ten. Rathbone's ticket was to Pentragon Bay.

"Seems to want to do it on the cheap," said the porter. "Hasn't got a sleeping berth anyway."

Carolus found a corner seat on the platform side in a compartment near the back of the train, from which he presently saw Rathbone go by. He waited until the train was out of London before he started on his way down the corridor, and then did so with the greatest caution. The train was far from full. There was no great rush to Cornwall in January and Sunday was not the most popular day for travelling. When Carolus eventually came on Rathbone, he saw that there were two others in the compartment, all three having taken corner seats.

He was uncomfortably hungry, for he had eaten nothing since breakfast at Coleshill Lodge, and now went to the Restaurant Car for tea and a quantity of buttered toast. As he returned to his place, he looked in at Rathbone's compartment, the whereabouts of which he had carefully noted, and saw that not only had he disappeared, but that the suitcase which he had brought from Barnes and which had been on the rack over his head had gone, too.

Since the train had not stopped, Carolus felt no dismay, but began another long walk through the corridor in search of his man. When he eventually found him, it was with a shock of surprise and something like admiration. The Anthony Eden hat, the sharp, white moustache, the neat suit were gone, and Rathbone sat alone in a compartment near the engine, clean-shaven, wearing corduroys and a beret and smoking a large pipe. Evidently he had assumed a character suitable to his future surroundings.

A writer? Painter? Hand-press printer? Someone, anyway, who would fit into the art colony of Pentragon Bay. On that train he was already far less noticeable than he had been as Colonel Hood.

So this escape route had been long prepared. Perhaps he had hired a studio or a bungalow on the cliffs. Perhaps he had manuscripts or an easel waiting for him. What name, Carolus wondered facetiously, would he adopt this time? Stephen something or would it be Evelyn? Did he intend to spend the rest of his life eating saffron cake and talking about Francis Bacon or Christopher Fry? At any rate he was safe enough where he was. No need to watch him till they approached Cornwall. He could not be going anywhere else in that rig. Carolus would be able to have dinner and sleep in peace tonight, knowing that Graham Auden or Angus Ruark or Benjamin Tynan or whoever it was would be safely there in the morning.

And he was. When Carolus wandered along half an hour before the train would reach Pentragon, Rathbone had already started a conversation—surely about Laurence Durrell or the Russian theatre or Henry Moore—with a noisily dressed character wearing a red beard. It was certainly an effective disguise which he had assumed in the train lavatory yesterday. Nothing in itself artificial. No false hair or color or anything difficult to maintain. He had shaved his moustache, combed his hair so that it spread from under the beret, and changed his clothes—nothing else. Yet Colonel Hood had ceased to exist and Sacheverel Amis, or what-not, sat in his place. In the region to which he was travelling, one might as well look for a needle in a bottle of hay as seek one artistic or literary character among the rest.

The difficulty for Carolus would come at Pentragon station. There would perhaps not be many to alight and Carolus in his quiet suit would stand out from the bearded throng. It was essential now that Rathbone should not recognize him. Rathbone must be left in the serenest of false security in his new home. Carolus asked a passing ticket-collector what was the next stop after Pentragon Bay and found it was Polstock Head, which lay by road only ten miles beyond it. He decided to remain in the train and return in the evening to Pentragon Bay. This would allow Rathbone time, perhaps, to give an indication of where he intended to stay.

He lunched at the Tredinnick Arms and drove back in the late afternoon to Pentragon. He decided to chance going into the Porthaziel Hotel, the only local pub, in the hope of gaining the information he wanted without revealing his presence in the town. He glanced uneasily at the customers, as well he might—they looked like a party of moujiks about to blow up a landowner's home or produce a balalaika and start stamping. But Rathbone was not among them. Conversation was emphatic and gesticulatory.

"One cannot dogmatize about non-objective art," Carolus heard.

"The stellar purity of Poliakoff," said a shriller voice.

"The spacelessness of Malevick," brought in a bass rumble.

"May I have a whisky and soda, please?" asked Carolus humbly.

The landlord looked on him as on a brother and moved up to the corner where Carolus stood, leaving his barmaid to serve the drinks.

"Cold, isn't it?" he said, with a marked determination to keep the conversation to its accepted course as between landlord and customer.

"It *is* cold," said Carolus.

"You'll excuse me, but you're not a painter, are you?"

"No."

"Nor yet a sculptor?"

"I'm not."

"You don't make things with wire and plasticine and old doorhandles and call 'em female figures?"

"I don't."

The landlord looked approvingly at him, then asked more anxiously: "Not a writer, are you? No poetry or anything like that?"

"None."

"Hand-printing? Woodcuts? Anything in that line?"

"No."

"Not music, is it?"

"I'm not in the least artistic, I'm afraid."

"Well, have a drink with me," invited the landlord.

"I don't mind," said Carolus, giving his answer in the traditional form.

"Hark at 'em!" said the landlord. Carolus did.

"Not that Berg's *Wozzeck* can be considered anything but bourgeois . . ." he heard.

"I see a certain affinity between Tippett and Tchelitchev."

"Not Mussorgsky. Not *Khovantschina*."

"Oh, God! Oh, Montreal!" said the landlord.

"Get many visitors at this time of year?" asked Carolus, keeping to accepted channels.

"They never stop. Oh, you mean in the hotel. No. We could do with a few more. I had a bit of bad luck this morning. There was one turned up from town. Admittedly he wore a beret and corduroys, but I didn't think he looked as though he'd be quite such a pain in the arse as this lot. When he got talking, I mean. Came off the London train and had a suitcase so I thought he meant to stay. He was just going to book a room when one of these—looked like the bearded lady at the fair—offered to let him his studio."

"Disappointing."

"Telling me. 'I have Penzanvoze Cottage,' says this one who wanted a shave; 'I was thinking of going down to Torremolinos for a few months.' The one who'd got off the train said his name was Osbert Auden and asked what the rent would be and, before I knew where I was, he'd taken the place and gone off there, suitcase and all. What do you think of that?"

"Irritating. Have a drink?"

"Thanks. I need it."

So did Carolus. "Panache", he heard, "Ustinov", "Beatniks", "Bertrand Russell", "empiricism", "polymorphism", "Sitwell",

"Perelman", "epistemology", "Simenon", "Blomdahl", "tonality", "Janacek", and "Heron". But he had the information he wanted.

He asked the landlord whether he could have a room for the night, to leave by an early train in the morning.

"Yes, certainly."

"I wonder whether I could possibly get out of this crowd," said Carolus, who feared that Rathbone might come in. The landlord was sympathetic.

"I don't blame you. I've had two years of it and I'm getting back to the Smoke. You never know there when you're going to be run in for keeping a disorderly house, but at least you don't have to listen to this lot. Yes, there's a little sitting-room with a fire in it at the top of the stairs where you can get a bit of peace. The wife's away at the moment. You'd like something to eat, I expect?"

Carolus followed the landlord, leaving a murmur of polysyllables and momentarily popular names.

Next morning, before a beard was in evidence, he walked to the station and caught his train. He realized as he travelled back to London that he had been lucky. He had gone on saying that, whenever Rathbone was wanted, he could be found, but was it true? One more in this *galère* would rouse no attention. It might well have taken the police weeks to run him to earth. But safely in Carolus's pocket-case was the note "Osbert Auden, Penzanvoze Cottage, Pentragon Bay, Cornwall". Carolus could now return to Newminster and await developments. It would not be long before a dentist had identified that skull so that now at least Carolus had a corpse to deal with—or all that mattered of a corpse.

15

As soon as he entered his home, he realized that something was very much amiss. It was not just a reproachful or a baffled look which Mrs Stick gave him, but one of real anger and despair. He was accustomed to her being put out by visitors connected with his cases, even to her threatening to leave if he became involved in "those nasty murders", but he had never seen the little woman look so ominously fierce as now. She said nothing till he was comfortably settled by the fire then she brought out her ultimatum:

"I'm sorry, sir, but we must give you a month's notice. And if you could find anyone else in the meantime, we should be glad."

"What's the matter, Mrs Stick?"

"You know very well what's the matter, sir. We ought never to have stayed on after the last time."

"But I *don't* know," said Carolus truthfully.

"Scotland Yard this time. It was bad enough when it was the police from round here and everyone knowing they was in and out. This one's got Criminal Investigation Department on his card."

"Is that more serious?"

"You'll excuse me, sir, but you're very well aware it's serious. For all me and Stick was to know, he's come to take you for interfering with things that are no concern of yours. He said he'd be back at five o'clock this afternoon, and I'm sure I don't know where to put myself for asking what he's coming for. Then there's my married sister to think of. She always seems to hear of anything like this and it causes Talk. I told you the last time, sir, we should have to go and now we shall. I'm sure neither Stick nor me would ever have wanted to leave you otherwise, but if there's one thing I don't like it's murder."

"I do so agree with you," said Carolus. "And what little I can do to defeat it I do."

"I'm not saying your intentions aren't good, sir, but it's the Talk. I was only saying to Stick, they'll say we're murderers next. No, sir, I'm very sorry, but this time we've made up our minds."

The bell rang. "There you are!" said Mrs Stick. "My heart jumps into my mouth every time I hear it. I suppose this is that policeman again."

Detective Inspector Mullard of New Scotland Yard was an altogether new kind of policeman for Carolus. Tall, grey-haired, businesslike, he had, as Carolus learnt later, risen to be a Major in SIB during the war. He had a domineering manner and was evidently accustomed to dealing with people who were in awe of him.

"Mr Deene? I have been trying to get in touch with you for two days. Mr Colin Humbell of Coleshill Lodge, Bolderton, gave me your name."

"Oh, yes. Do sit down."

"I gathered from him that you had suggested removing the floor of his summer-house and digging there. May I ask why, Mr Deene?"

"Curiosity," said Carolus. He had decided to fence a little till Mullard could see that his own position was not impregnable.

"I see. You realize, of course, that what you have been doing comes very near to obstructing the police?"

"I realize nothing of the sort. I have already given you considerable assistance and may be prepared to assist you further. But not if you adopt this somewhat hectoring manner."

"I believe you consider yourself a private investigator of some kind?"

"I am a schoolmaster interested in criminology."

"You think that warrants your interference in a very grave case like this? From what I have heard, you may well be charged with complicity."

Carolus smiled.

"Really, Inspector, you've mistaken your man. Let's stop talking like two politicians at a summit meeting and come to realities. I'm interested in this case and I've no wish to keep any information to myself. It has, in fact, reached a stage where there's nothing much more I can do. Getting convictions is police work."

Mullard seemed to consider.

"Look at it from my point of view," he said. "I'm handed a case. Woman's skull unearthed in a garden at Bolderton . . ."

"So it *was* a woman's skull."

Mullard ignored this.

"Previous occupant of the house recently disappeared with his wife, leaving talk in a Kentish village. A nasty-looking case and one on which I should want to concentrate everything I've got. Then what do I find? The skull has been unearthed at the suggestion of a private investigator who had kept watch in the house on the previous night and seen a woman enter the garden. Moreover, I find on inquiry that you were in occupation of the country cottage from which Rathbone disappeared at the time when the local CID were searching it. You must own it's an absurd situation."

"I don't see it. If I wanted to hold back relevant information—was in fact one of these honor-and-glory boys one reads about—I can see it would be tiresome; but I'm not. I'll tell you anything you like that I know about the people in this case. My position is quite unequivocal. I was asked by a relative to discover what had happened to a woman called Anne Rathbone, formerly Anne Bright. I have discovered. What remains of her is on your desk at the Yard, a particularly nasty-looking skull. You had no difficulty in identifying it?"

"I'll ask any questions that are going to be asked, Mr Deene. How did you know it would be buried at Bolderton?"

"Now you're asking me not about the case but about my own simple methods. That, I'm afraid, won't do."

It was clear that Mullard had the greatest difficulty in controlling his temper, but he was intelligent enough to see that it would pay him. After a silence he said rather grudgingly: "Yes. As a matter of fact it was Anne Rathbone's skull. Her dentist was able to tell us that. Expert opinion gives it more than five years underground. Now, perhaps, you can tell me where I can find Rathbone?"

"Yes, I can do that. He is masquerading as an artist or writer or something under the name of Osbert Auden. He has taken Penzanvoze Cottage at Pentragon Bay in Cornwall. He was certainly there yesterday. But I don't know what he is using for money."

"He drew his lot at Folkestone. Quite a considerable sum. I won't ask you how you know he's in Cornwall, but what's this about masquerading?"

"Just taking the color of his surroundings. If you want to look like a member of a Cornish art colony, you don't wear a pin-stripe suit. His last impersonation was of Colonel Hood, a very spruce military gentleman. He has a mobile sort of face and by simply shaving his moustache and pulling his hair down under his beret and putting on corduroys in the train lavatory he became a new man. He was fond of amateur theatricals once, you know."

"I didn't know. I have only just been given this case," said Mullard aggrievedly. "So you think we can arrest him there?"

"If you want to arrest him, yes."

"Of course I want to arrest him. He'll be convicted for sure."

"That depends on the charge," said Carolus mildly.

But Mullard paid no attention to this.

"Do you mind if I use your telephone?" he asked.

Carolus showed him where it was and carefully closed the door on him. He could guess what call Mullard wished to make and he did not think it would do much to pacify Mrs Stick if she heard instructions to arrest a man for murder.

"Anne Rathbone is only the beginning of this," he observed coolly when Mullard returned. "What do you intend to do about the other women?"

"I hope you're not being funny, Mr Deene, because I find this case far from funny. The other *women?*"

"For the sake of convenience I have thought of them as the first, second and third Mrs Rathbone. They'll have to be traced, won't they?"

"If you mean the woman who was with him at Bluefield, our people have known for some time that she wasn't the one he originally married. But you said 'women'."

"Yes. I was thinking of the second Mrs Rathbone. The Hastings one."

"You'd better tell me about that," said Mullard ungraciously. Carolus did.

"This is pretty dreadful," said Mullard. "Another of these Christie cases." Then he asked as though he feared the answer: "Any more?"

"I think we had better have a drink," said Carolus. "Scotch?"

"Thanks."

"I don't know whether there are any more. Anne Rathbone had a sister who seems to have died rather suddenly. She was on the streets."

He told Mullard about Frenchy. Mullard made a sound which could fairly be described as a groan.

"The father, Herbert Bright, tried to prevent Rathbone marrying Anne. He also died suddenly. Ptomaine poisoning was given as the cause, I believe."

While Mullard was taking notes of these details, Carolus added, "You know that Rathbone was once employed by Tonkins Sons and Company. They are wholesale chemists."

"Yes, I knew that," said Mullard, writing busily. "I should be glad to hear anything else you may have to tell me."

Carolus told him about Mrs Chalk, the villagers' recollections at Bluefield, Mumford the solicitor and his clerk, Miss Ramble's curious reminiscences, "Old Maree" and Elizabeth, Villiers, the Lascelles Private Hotel and Mrs Richards. He talked slowly enough for Mullard to make his notes.

"I suppose I ought to say I'm grateful to you," said the Inspector. "I should have come to all this in time, but it will save me some work."

Carolus did not, however, mention Sloane Gillick. For one thing, the police would have investigated the question of fingerprints; for another he did not want to cause trouble for Gillick, whose position as a private consultant now that he had retired might not be approved by Mullard and others in office. Nor did he mention Mrs Myberg because, not having talked to her yet, he did not know whether her information would be useful. Moreover, Carolus gave no opinion of his own nor hint of how he saw the case. He had undertaken to tell Mullard such facts as he knew and he did so. He then thought it was time to venture on a few questions of his own.

"You say that Rathbone withdrew the money he had in the Folkestone bank. This would include, presumably, the sum he received for his wife's life interest in the capital left by her father?"

"Yes. We have only just got the handwriting-boys on to the signature of 'Anne Rathbone' which has been used for the last six years, but there can be no possible doubt (in view of the identification of the skull) that it is a forgery."

"I see."

"It was an easy signature to forge, I understand. Anne had almost childish handwriting."

"Would you get your people to compare it with the signature used at Mumford's office? I should be interested to know whether they were forged by the same hand."

Mullard made another note.

"Was anything else found under the summer-house at Coleshill Lodge?"

"Nothing. It isn't a pleasant thought, but we think the remainder of the body was burnt. There have been cases of that, you know, in which the skull has not been included. There were no houses near the Lodge when the Rathbones lived there and the destruction of most of a body by fire would present no great difficulty."

"Not, as you say, a pleasant thought."

"Mind you our people haven't been idle, Mr Deene. We have a fairly complete record of Rathbone's life up to the time of his marriage."

"That must be interesting."

"It's not quite what you would expect. He was born in 1908 at Lewisham, the only son of a fairly prosperous chemist who was also a Deacon at a local chapel called the Tabernacle of Mount Sion Reformed. His mother was a woman of strong character who dominated his early life. When Brigham Rathbone was fourteen, she died and left him without the support, guidance and discipline to which he was accustomed. His father was remote and far too old for him, and there seems to have been no other relatives or close friends of the family. Most of this information, by the way, comes from a very intelligent woman, now the welfare officer of an immense concern, who was brought up in the same street as Rathbone. Their parents were either next-door neighbors or very near it.

"So Rathbone, left without the strong hand of his mother, drifted into a sort of inertia. He was at a large Secondary School then, but was expelled for cheating in a public examination. Rather harsh, you may think, but he had been in trouble several times before. He became a weak and rather timid kind of loafer. His father made several attempts to get him to work for himself or others, but they were not successful. This seems to have continued for some years till his father decided to retire. He sold the shop for a very modest sum in 1927 and lived only five years more. He left almost everything to the Tabernacle of Mount Sion Reformed, and Rathbone found himself, for the first time in his life, under the necessity of working.

"One thing that seems to emerge from all this is that, when the fellow needed for his own comfort to get something done, he could do it. He was bone-lazy but not altogether incompetent. He went to the firm which had been his father's chief suppliers, Tonkins Sons and Company, and secured a job for himself. It was a comfortable rather old-fashioned business, and Rathbone, who managed to avoid war service on medical grounds, remained there, just keeping his job with the minimum effort, for fourteen years till he married Anne Bright."

"It's not a very inspiring record, is it?" commented Carolus. "I should like to hold it up to some of my pupils as an 'awful example of laziness in boyhood', ending as it has."

Mullard accepted another drink. He was considerably mellowed not by the whisky but by Carolus's readiness to give him information and particularly, Carolus thought, for enabling him to arrest Rathbone.

"What I want to ask you about," he said confidentially, "is the woman in the garden at Bolderton. Who was she, Deene?"

"I could not see her face," said Carolus. "I just saw her disappearing into the shrubbery."

"Tall or short?"

"Impossible to say. I had only the moonlight to see by and that was not the sparkling clear moonlight of a frosty night. But there is something which may help you in this. The proprietress of the Lascelles Private Hotel told me that 'Colonel Hood' had been visited on several occasions lately by a woman."

"I see," said Mullard making another note. "And you think it is the same one who entered the garden?"

"Surely what I think can't be of much help to you, Inspector?"

"No, I suppose not. But you must have some opinion about the identity of the woman in the garden?"

"Oh, yes, I have. But I want to give you facts, not opinions. The facts here are that I just saw female attire and could not see more; but there is something that may help you. A car was waiting round the corner; I heard it driven away."

"A taxi, you think?"

"Can't say. But it would be an odd sort of taxi that would go all the way out to Bolderton in the small hours and wait in a residential street while its fare disappeared round the corner for a while."

"When I said a taxi," Mullard argued, "I meant a hired car of some kind. Rathbone's car, as you know, was left abandoned in London when he first disappeared. If he was driving that night, he must have hired one."

"Then you don't need me to tell you that it can easily be traced."

"Not easily, Mr Deene. All these things take time and trouble. Our men are overworked as it is. But it probably can be traced."

"Just as with your resources and authority you could get further details of the death of Lucille French at 16b, Montgolfier Street, five years ago."

"I suppose we could, if we had any reason to do so."

"You see, Inspector, our points of view are fundamentally different. You want to convict Rathbone of the murder of Anne and hang him for it. You may be quite right in the usual view that a man can only hang once, so one murder's enough to convict him of. But I'm a congenitally inquisitive person. I want to know all about the second and third Mrs Rathbone, if you'll forgive the loose terminology. I want to know about Frenchy. I don't want there to be a factual question about the case I can't answer."

"That's all right," said Mullard, rising. "Only keep out of my hair. I've got a tough job, as you know. I don't say I'm not grateful to you, but I've got to get down to realities."

"Quite. By the way, before you go you can do me a small favor. I'll get my housekeeper to show you out. You might tell her you came to consult me about sending your son to the Queen's School or wanted to discuss a point of history or a chess problem, or that we were in the army together. Whatever seems most probable to you. She gave me notice when she saw your card."

Mullard smiled. "I'll see what I can do," he said. When Mrs Stick appeared, Carolus realized that in this at least the detective was not without ingenuity.

"I wasn't to know that was one of the boys' fathers, was I, sir? It's what's happened before makes me think things. And fancy him wanting you to give his son special coaching! Mr Hollingbourne won't like *that*, will he? I'm sorry if I spoke Hasty, but it's the Talk we're so afraid of. I suppose the man can't help being in the police, but it does give us a bad name, their calling here. Still, this time there's no bones broken, is there? Now I've got a nice omelette oaks sham pig nons for you with a rag out de buff to follow."

16

BEFORE Carolus could enjoy that delectable meal, he had another caller. Hurrying in from the very cold night, Mr Gorringer, if not like Nature red in tooth and claw, was scarlet in ears and nose. His protuberant eyes were wide with alarm.

"Have you seen the evening paper?" he asked, over-acting his distraction.

"Not yet. Have a drink, Headmaster?"

"Seldom as I indulge, Deene, I feel that on this occasion I need heartening. It was an ill day in which Mrs Gorringer suggested to her relative by marriage that she should consult you. You will be shocked to know that the police have discovered human remains in the house at Bolderton in which this fiend in human form, Rathbone, once lived."

"In the garden, not the house. Under the rubbish-heap."

"You knew that the discovery had been made?"

"I made it."

"Ah, Deene, what ghosts have you raised, far better left undisturbed? What odious things have you brought to light?"

"Just a skull," said Carolus maddeningly.

"At least I have cause to be thankful that the press so far make no reference to your part in the discovery of this hecatomb. Perhaps you can further reassure me. Have they been able to apprehend the villain responsible?"

"I should think Rathbone is already under arrest. He will be brought up from Cornwall tomorrow."

"He had taken refuge in Cornwall, had he? But the long arm of the law has sought him out? Then I assume he will be brought to justice and condemned without any further participation by you in the matter?"

"I don't know whether he will be condemned. It depends on the charge."

"But no testimony by you will be required, Deene? It is that which most disturbs me."

"I shouldn't think so. The tenant of Coleshill Lodge can give evidence of finding the skull."

"I breathe again. When I read the news this evening I was quite *tracassé*. I feared that the good name of the school was in jeopardy and this time, though indirectly, through my own fault."

Without asking Mr Gorringer, Carolus mixed him another dry martini and the headmaster permitted himself to relax.

"So now," he observed, "we can prepare ourselves for the coming term with no more of these morbid distractions."

"Morbid? I suppose so. But deeply interesting. A great many questions remain unanswered yet. We have discovered the remains of Anne Rathbone. What about the others?"

"The *others*?"

"The women Rathbone lived with at Hastings and Bluefield respectively. Also Charlotte Bright, the sister of the woman buried at Bolderton? Where are these?" asked Carolus, catching the headmaster's trick of rhetorical question.

"You do not surely mean to involve yourself farther, my dear Deene? Your task is done. You have rendered a great service to the children of Mrs Chalk, who will now inherit what was rightfully theirs some years ago. What mystery, then, remains?"

"Everything, almost. I like to get at the truth. As a matter of fact, I am pretty near it now. I have to see one other person and I think the whole thing will fit into place."

"I wash my hands of it," boomed Mr Gorringer. "What good purpose do you serve? If this ghoul is guilty of more murders, you cannot bring the unfortunate women back to life. To use a phrase more appropriate to Mrs Gorringer, you have your skull, why worry with your cross-bones?"

"Sorry to be a bore on the point, Headmaster, but what I want is the truth."

"You are incorrigible, Deene. You have solved the crux of the problem. Must I suspect you of wishing to adorn your theory till you can give us a dramatic *mise-en-scène*, as on other occasions? Ah, well, I have learned my lesson. If a thousand relatives by marriage of Mrs Gorringer are deprived of their inheritance, I shall not give my consent to application being made to you. Now I must return to the family fireside."

"Mrs Chalk still with you?"

A graver look crossed Mr Gorringer's features. "It appears," he said rather gloomily, "that she will remain so until her return to Brazil. I feel that she has given a somewhat liberal interpretation to our invitation to spend Christmas with us. Her husband has already returned to Rio de Janeiro. Well, Deene, I mustn't keep you from your researches."

On the following morning Carolus left for Bayswater, hoping for his long-promised interview with Mrs Myberg, formerly "Cara", who had been the friend of "Frenchy". In the London Telephone Directory he had found the address of a Maurice Myberg at 17, Marie Louise Avenue, W.2, and felt safe in supposing that it was what he wanted. The house was one of those ugly stucco monsters built a century ago for prosperous city men and fallen on poorer days. There were three bells beside the door and he pressed the top one, labelled Myberg, glad of the heavy portico which shielded him from observation from an upper window. After ringing three times at intervals of several minutes, he was about to turn away when the door was opened by a hastily dressed woman who looked as though she had just crawled from a bed in which she had spent a sleepless night. Even before either of them spoke, Carolus had the impression that she was desperately anxious. A few moments later he knew that she was afraid.

"Mrs Myberg?"

"Yes."

"Mrs Cara Myberg, I think?"

The name brought something—guilt, fear, mere nervousness?—to her eyes.

"Well?"

"I should like to speak to you."

"What . . . about?"

"A private matter. I have your address from a woman known as Maree. No, don't try to shut the door. That would be very silly. I want no more than a few minutes' conversation."

She hesitated but, after a glance about her, indicated that Carolus should enter. She led the way upstairs to the door of a flat which she had left open. "What is it?" she said suspiciously.

Carolus examined her carefully. She was a woman of perhaps fifty years with dyed hair and a somewhat raddled face. There was no doubt about it she was very much afraid. He decided to go straight into the attack.

"Do you know a man called Rathbone?" he asked sharply.

"Yes. Well, just by name, that is. I've heard him mentioned. Why? Who are you?"

"I'm not a policeman."

"You don't need to tell me that. I can smell coppers a mile off. Who are you then?"

"My name's Deene. I'm looking for a woman called Bright."

"She's dead. Haven't you seen in the papers? They've just found her remains at Bolderton."

"That was Anne Bright who became Anne Rathbone. I'm looking for Charlotte Bright."

"She's dead, too."

"How do you know?"

" . . . I knew her in the old days."

"But you'd left her before she moved to Montgolfier Street and died there—or hadn't you?"

"Of course I had. Years before."

"Where were you at the time?"

"I don't know what it's to do with you or who you may be to come asking me questions."

"Just a friend of the family. I am authorized by Mrs Chalk, as a matter of fact."

"Oh, that bitch! What's she got to do with it? She scarcely knew Anne."

"Charlotte told you that?"

"Yes. Charlotte told me all about her family."

"How long did you know her?"

"I don't know to a day. Some years, anyway. Till I went off."

"With your present husband?"

"No. It wasn't, if you want to know. It was before I'd met him."

"When *did* you meet him?"

Mrs Myberg thought for a moment.

"Oh, some time ago. After I'd left this other chap."

"Whose name was?"

"What's that got to do with it? I thought it was Charlotte Bright you wanted to know about?"

"It was. It is. When did you hear of her death?"

"Must have been soon after it happened."

"How did you hear?"

"I forget now. Someone must have told me. These things get passed round."

"Was it after you'd married Myberg?"

"No. Before. I was still at . . . Birmingham."

"You nearly made a mistake about the name of that place, didn't you, Mrs Myberg?"

"I don't know what you mean."

Her defiance was defensive, the defiance of a cornered animal.

"What are you holding back?"

"Nothing. I knew Charlotte. 'Frenchy' we used to call her."

"What did she look like?"

There was another pause.

"Tall and slender. Long neck. Lovely eyes."

"What caused her death?"

"It was a mystery at the time. The doctor gave a certificate, of course, but they nearly always do with girls like that. Don't want to be bothered, I suppose. I always thought there was something funny about her going so suddenly, but you can't tell."

"How was she identified?"

"Why . . ." Carolus thought for a moment he had broken down the witness. But she rallied. "Why, her sister came and identified her, I believe. I wasn't there. That's what I've heard."

"Which sister?"

"Anne, of course. Must have been Anne. I never heard of any other sister."

"But Anne had been dead four years, if the skull just found was hers."

Mrs Myberg blinked. "So she had. I never thought of that. Well, whoever it was identified her as Charlotte Bright, and she was allowed to be cremated."

"You seem to know a lot about it, considering that at the time you were living in . . . Birmingham, wasn't it? With someone whose name you don't want to mention."

"She was my friend. Naturally I wanted to find out all about it afterwards. I wish I knew what all this is about. I should like to know what you're driving at."

"When did you see Rathbone last?" said Carolus, returning to his original line of attack.

"I don't know that I've ever seen him."

"You started by telling me you knew him."

"Only by name, I said. Charlotte used to talk about him."

"Oh, she knew him then?"

"Yes. She went down there once when Anne was ill."

"To Hastings?"

"Hastings?" said Mrs Myberg, obviously startled by the name. "No. Bolderton it was."

"She never went to see them at Hastings?"

"Not that I know of. I never knew they lived at Hastings. I thought Charlotte said Bolderton."

"So if it wasn't her sister who lived with Rathbone at Hastings, Charlotte would never have known of it?"

"I suppose not. I don't really know. I didn't hear all that much from Charlotte about her family. She wasn't crazy about any of them. Anne got all her father's money."

"Not quite all, surely?"

"That thousand pounds, you mean? Well, that came from her mother, really. Her mother had about that when she died, and asked for it to go to Charlotte one day."

"That must have been before you knew Charlotte, surely? Her father died in the last year of the war."

"Must have been, then."

"She must have told you about it?"

"Must have."

"You have a good memory, Mrs Myberg."

"Yes. I've always been told I have."

"Yet you don't remember meeting Rathbone."

"I've told you, I never knew him." She watched him with an open-eyed, mesmerized stare of sheer panic.

"But you know Colonel Hood, I think?"

Carolus could see that this was "a hit, a very palpable hit". It took Mrs Myberg several seconds to pull herself together sufficiently to say: "No. Who's he?"

"You never visited the Lascelles Private Hotel?"

"Never heard of it. I don't really know what you're getting at. All I've got to do with this is that I knew Charlotte Bright before her death."

"You think she is dead, then?"

"Dead? Of course she's dead. You can see the record of it if you doubt that."

"Oh, I don't doubt that the woman who called herself Lucille French, who lived in Montgolfier Street, is dead. I was remembering that there was no proof that she was in reality Charlotte Bright."

"But they found her papers and her sister identified her."

"Someone calling herself Mrs Rathbone identified her. Charlotte's sister was dead."

"I see what you mean. But it must have been Charlotte Bright. Frenchy always told me that was her real name. And she couldn't have made up all that about her father and sister and everything."

"No, she couldn't; but I should like to find someone who knew her as a girl, all the same. Just to make sure she was tall and slim and long-necked."

"You seem very interested in all this. I wish you'd tell me what you're after and why you want to know."

"I will. I'm after the truth. I want to know because I started to investigate and shan't rest until I have the whole thing clear."

"But you're not the Law."

"No. That's perhaps why I'm keener on these details. The police will be able to get them from Rathbone now they've arrested him."

Watching carefully, Carolus saw that this had gone home, but the woman had been prepared for something of the sort and kept her head. "You mean, because they've found Anne's body?"

"I don't know yet what he will be charged with. I imagine it depends on what comes out during his interrogation."

Mrs Myberg had an ashen-grey look. She looked as though she might be sick. There was a heavy silence in the room, then she asked: "Where was Rathbone when they arrested him?"

"I wonder why you want to know that. You've never met the man, you say."

"I just wondered. Anyone would wonder after reading in the paper about what they've found at Bolderton."

"He was in Cornwall, pretending to be an artist called Osbert Auden."

"Oh, is that where he was? I went down to Cornwall once, years ago. I didn't like it."

"No?"

"No, I didn't. So you think the police will get a lot of information out of Rathbone?"

"Yes. They're expert at that."

"About his wife, you mean?"

"Anne? Yes. Partly that. But he has lived with two other women who are missing. They'll want to trace those."

Mrs Myberg lit a cigarette. "Oh, I didn't know that."

"Tell me, do you think there was anything between him and Charlotte Bright?"

"Frenchy? Oh, I shouldn't think so. So far as I know she only saw him that once when she went down there."

"You don't think he ever went to Montgolfier Street?"

"I wouldn't know. Frenchy and I never wrote to one another. Well, you don't, do you? But she certainly never said anything to me about him when I knew her, except just that she couldn't understand why her sister had married him. It seemed he lived on her money altogether. Never *would* work."

"She told you that?"

"Yes. I remember her telling me that."

"What I was hoping you would be able to tell me, Mrs Myberg, was whether she had any notion of what happened at Bolderton. After all, she only had to go down to Hastings for a day to see that the woman whom Rathbone was calling his wife was not her sister Anne."

"She may have, for all I know. I'd gone off by then."

"By when?"

"Well, soon after she went down to visit them at Bolderton. I never knew about Hastings and I never saw Frenchy again. My life changed altogether, you see."

"Yes."

"You think I shall have the Law asking me all this?"

"I don't know what the police will ask you."

"I don't see how they'll ever know about me. After all, it's six years since I left Frenchy. I've been married for three."

"They're sure to pick up 'Old Maree'."

"*She'll* tell them, the lousy old grass! Same as she told you."

"Yes, I think she will. But you surely won't mind giving them the little information you have?"

"It's not me. It's my husband. Morry hates anything like that. Still, so long as they come when he's out . . ."

"I shouldn't count on that. They may want to ask him something."

Mrs Myberg looked sick again. Carolus could see the fear in her eyes. It could, of course, be fear of losing security, but he thought it was something else.

"Whatever could they want to know from *him?*" she asked in a strangled voice.

"I don't know how their minds work. I just thought it possible."

"It's nothing to do with him! I won't have them asking him questions. Or you either. Perhaps *you* want to ask him something?"

"I do, as a matter of fact."

"What? You've asked me enough. What do you want to get on to him for? He never even set eyes on Frenchy or Montgolfier Street, or anything. He's straight, is Morry. Straight as a die. I can't think why you should want to worry him."

Carolus stood up. "It's not really important," he said.

"What the hell is it?"

"Don't bother yourself. I don't suppose I shall need to ask him at all."

"But what *is* it? You can tell me that before you go. I've answered your questions enough. What *do* you want to know from Morry?"

"Where he met you," said Carolus, and left her with her large mouth agape and her eyes quite frantic. He was glad to reach the open air, heavy with a damp chill as it was. He found a light fog in the southern suburbs but, as he neared Newminster, it was clear and bright. His interrogations were over.

17

HE was surprised, on his return, to have a phone message from Mullard asking whether it would be possible for Carolus to call and see him tomorrow.

"We've got your man," said Mullard when Carolus was in his office next morning; "but our people down there are a bit worried. He claims to know nothing whatever about it. I thought, as you know him by sight, you might come down to Pentragon with me."

"Yes, I will; provided you come in my car. I can make it in six hours, or seven at the most, if we get held up at all."

Mullard accepted this and they set off. They said little of the case on the way, Mullard because he felt he had already gone further than professional reserve allowed; Carolus because there was nothing more he wanted to know from Mullard. When they reached Pentragon, Carolus suggested a drink at the Porthaziel Hotel before getting down to business. The landlord was delighted to see him.

"You back already?" he said affably as he served their drinks. "You must like it. I'm damned if I do! I can't wait to get back to the Smoke. They never stop, you know, midday and night."

"The landlord is not an enthusiast about the arts," explained Carolus to Mullard.

"I don't know about arts," said the landlord. "This lot give me the ——s. Listen to 'em."

Carolus and Mullard did. "Nothing as *vieux jeu* as Eliot", they heard, "quasi-surréalism", "conceptual images", "Derain", "Harold Pinter", "Brecht", "flaccid as Lawrence", and one shrill pained *cri de coeur*—"You might as well say E. M. Forster!"

"It is rather overwhelming," agreed Carolus. "How did that chap get on? The one you were telling me about?"

"Which one was that?"

"The man who was going to take a room in your hotel and instead met the owner of Penzanvoze Cottage."

"Oh, that one. It was a funny thing about him. It seems he didn't take that cottage after all. Couldn't agree on terms, I dare say. Osbert Auden his name was."

"Yes, that's the man."

"No. He didn't take the cottage. Just as well perhaps, because the police have just nicked the owner of it."

"Really? What's his name?"

"God knows. All their names are alike to me. Christopher and Peter and Stephen and Francis." He turned to a beard near by. "What's the name of that bloke who had Penzanvoze Cottage? Just been nicked? Oscar Gordon. That's it. Oscar Gordon his name is."

"What was he arrested for?" asked Carolus, conscious of Mullard fuming beside him.

"No one seems to know. Usual thing I suppose, with these bees. It seems the London police wanted him. Anyhow, he's inside now. Took him in yesterday afternoon, I heard."

"What about the other one?"

"The one who was going to take the cottage? He's gone."

"Does anyone know where?"

"No. Just went. He was in here last night and heard this Oscar Gordon was nicked. Not been seen since."

"Come on," said Mullard to Carolus.

They went round to the police station, where a worried Inspector awaited them.

"He's roaring to beat the band," the Inspector told Mullard. "Screaming blue murder for solicitors. Shouting about wrongful arrest. Every time I go near he yells *habeas corpus* at me. I don't know what to do with him."

"I'm not surprised. You've got the wrong man."

"You said one of these artistic crackpots at Penzanvoze Cottage."

"I said Osbert Auden."

"This one's Oscar Gordon. It sounded like that on the phone. He lives at Penzanvoze Cottage. And he's artistic, all right. Beard, jeans, the lot."

"I might have known," said Mullard, "I should never have listened to an amateur. I should have come down here myself. Can't leave anything to anyone else. Now you're in for a nice case of wrongful arrest, Inspector. There'll be Members of Parliament popping up all over the House about this."

"I arrested the man living at Penzanvoze Cottage, just as you said," returned the Inspector sulkily.

"But the name!" said Mullard, clinging to his strong point.

"They've all got names like that. There's an Osric Borden in the village. I might just as easily have thought you meant him."

"I meant the man I named and no one else. You'd better bring him in and let's see whether we can get over it."

"He's nasty, I don't mind telling you. You won't talk him round easily. Talks about Craig, Marwood and Podola. Screams about the Gestapo. Says this is a Police State!"

Mr Oscar Gordon was a small fiery man with an auburn beard and very heavy thick-lensed spectacles. He remained silent just long enough for Mullard to say he was from Scotland Yard and that there had been a grave and regrettable mistake; then, screwing up his face and releasing a deluge of saliva, he said, "Mistake? *Mistake?* You dare to talk to me about a mistake? Perhaps the Home Secretary will be able to explain *this* mistake! Perhaps he'll say that he acted on the best advice *this* time! I've been kept in a cell by your mistake and, by God, you're going to pay for it! I shall see my Member of Parliament. I shall write to *The Times*. I shall telephone the Chief Constable. I shall report this to every section of the press. I shall sue you in every Court in the country. I might have remained in that cell for years before you discovered your mistake. Look what happened to Oscar Slater through a mistake like that! Look what happened to Evans! It's infamous. You stand there calmly talking about a mistake!"

"By a most unfortunate chance, your name resembled that used by the man we wanted, Mr Gordon."

"So I must change my name, must I, to avoid being dragged to prison? My name, sir, is known to art lovers throughout the kingdom. Do you know I hold the silver medal of the Bodmin Etching Society? I have been hung in three Exhibitions by the New Penzance Group? How dare you talk about my name? Before many hours are past, you will realize the enormity of this deliberate attack on the rights of a citizen! Don't speak to me again! Don't attempt to excuse yourself! If there's any justice left in the land, I'll break every one of you!"

He was gone, leaving behind him "the icy silence of the tomb".

"Meanwhile," said Mullard presently, "where do you suppose we are going to find the man we want? Heaven knows he has had warning enough. I would point out to you, Inspector, that he is wanted on a charge of murder."

"I know that, Inspector," replied the local man tartly.

"You don't suppose he is waiting here for us to arrest him, do you?"

"I'll send a man to the railway station and check on the bus services."

"It's all you can do now. But please don't arrest the stationmaster or any of the bus-conductors."

"No need for sarcasm, Inspector. We carried out your instructions to the best of our ability."

When Mullard was alone with Carolus, he asked whether Carolus thought Rathbone would adopt another disguise.

"Quite likely. But his wardrobe must be giving out."

"You think, then, he'll return to 'Colonel Hood'?"

"Something like that."

"It may take weeks to find him now. He's got plenty of money in one-pound notes. Have you no suggestions?"

"Yes. A very cogent one. I suggest you put a twenty-four-hour-a-day watch on number 17, Marie Louise Avenue, Bayswater."

"Now, Mr Deene, this is no time for mystery and tricks. You can't make fools of the police, you know. I have been very patient with you and listened to a great deal of amateur theorizing; but don't go too far. Who lives at this address?"

"A woman called Cara Myberg."

"What's she to do with it?"

"She was a friend of another woman who called herself Lucille French and who died. I think I told you about Lucille French."

"Yes. Does this Myberg know Rathbone?"

"She says not."

"But you think?"

"I think you should have her very carefully watched."

"It's all very well, Mr Deene. I went on your information before and you see what has come of it."

"I told you that Rathbone was masquerading as a writer or artist at Pentragon under the name of Osbert Auden. I was right."

"But you also told me he had taken Penzanvoze Cottage, which was incorrect."

"Yes, I admit that. My information was through the landlord of the Porthaziel Hotel. He was positive, but I should have warned you that that piece of information was second-hand. You heard the landlord explain that the man had decided against it at the last moment."

"The consequences are very unpleasant. As you know, the police are not generally popular just now."

"You put it very mildly. But, forgetting that, I can tell you that my information about Mrs Myberg is first-hand. I interviewed her yesterday."

"I see. You think Rathbone will contact her?"

"Once again, you don't want to know what I think. As you have just crisply pointed out, I *thought* Rathbone had taken Penzanvoze Cottage and misled you over it. But, if I may suggest it, I would not leave that woman for a moment without a watch over the place."

Mullard was still inclined to grumble. "You laymen talk as though we had unlimited manpower resources. It will mean taking men from important duties."

"All right," said Carolus. "It's not my affair. Street betting, prostitution, public decency, illicit parking, drinking hours are doubtless of more importance. I can only throw out my little suggestion."

Mullard looked at him resentfully as though to imply a regret, a very bitter regret, that he had ever been brought into contact with Carolus. When they had returned to the hotel, however, Mullard disappeared for a long time into the telephone booth in the hall while Carolus went to the bar. Here he found Mr Oscar Gordon, a very waterspout of saliva and the center of a sympathetic group. Picasso, Sartre, even Dame Edith Sitwell, were forgotten as the small man said his piece.

"At last," he spat, "they called it a mistake. A *mistake*! Heads shall fall over this! There must be a fate in the name Oscar. It is the third of three infamously unjust imprisonments—Oscar Slater, Oscar Wilde and Oscar Gordon."

An irreverent voice came from a young man across the room: "Come off it, Gordon. You were only inside a few hours."

Oscar Gordon turned to the speaker, then said with chilly venom: "That is what I might expect from a man who does *woodcuts*. But we shall see!"

Carolus and Mullard decided to stay at the Porthaziel Hotel that night and leave very early in the morning. During the evening the local police inspector came in to give Mullard the results of his inquiries at the railway station and bus stop. These were simply stated. Both the booking clerk and a porter had noticed a man dressed in corduroys and a beret and carrying a suitcase who had boarded the London train yesterday evening. The porter, who was a customer at the Porthaziel Hotel, in fact remembered the man's arrival and knew that he had intended to take Penzanvoze Cottage. But this information was not very useful to Mullard, since the train stopped several times on the way up. The fact that Rathbone had bought a ticket to London might not mean anything at all. He was astute enough to realize that Gordon had been arrested in mistake for him, and therefore that his flight and disguise were known. He might have gone to London as providing him with the best chance of remaining undiscovered, or he might have chosen one of the southern towns through which they passed. Carolus had never been to Reading, for instance, but imagined it a city in which one could live unobserved for years.

Carolus turned in early, much to the regret of the landlord, who found his company refreshing.

The drive back to London was even less chatty than the drive down. Carolus realized, not without amusement, that Mullard had plenty to think about. He himself felt a blissful unconcern since the actual catching of criminals was a police task, not his. They had all the resources and would not hesitate to use them. The hunt was up, and Carolus, who had never been an enthusiast for blood sports, would take no part in it; but he could not help speculating on Rathbone's next impersonation. As he had pointed out to Mullard, Rathbone's wardrobe could not be unlimited, so it was reasonable to suppose that he would make some adaptation of a guise already used, and the most probable was Colonel Hood's neat dark suit. A clerical collar, perhaps? If it occurred to him he would scarcely be able to resist it.

Carolus dropped Mullard in Whitehall and drove back to New-minster. There would, he believed, be a pause of some days before any further developments were likely, and frankly he was glad of it. He wanted a rest. It had been an unsavory case at the best of times. He had taken it up without the enthusiasm he usually felt when an opportunity for investigation opened before him. At the time he had put this down to the fact that there was no clear case of murder and he had always said that he would never investigate anything else. But, as its grim implications became apparent, he felt more than that.

As usual, it had brought him into contact with good and like-able people, as well as a good many less agreeable. He thought of Mrs Luggett and Mr Toffins, of Mr and Mrs Humbell and sensible Mrs Richards. But he felt sick of the stale and morbid, the nasty little flat in which Cara Myberg lived, the pretentious Lascelles Private Hotel, the important Mr Villiers and all the neo-what-ever-they-were of Pentragon Bay. He wanted his own home and a few days in which to forget Glose Cottage and the limp lace at Miss Ramble's skinny neck.

He garaged his car with some relief, for five hundred miles in two days was a lot of motoring on English roads. And this time, to his great relief, Mrs Stick welcomed him with the prim movement of her lips which she meant for a smile. In a few minutes Carolus was deep in his armchair with a whisky and soda beside him and a cigar from which he blew slow, luxurious puffs. Mrs Stick brought him the evening paper, and it was without rancor that she said: "There. A cigar before dinner. You'll never enjoy the pullet à la cream I've got for you. I was only saying to Stick, cigars are for after dinner. But there you are."

"No telephone calls, Mrs Stick?"

"No. Was you expecting one?"

"Not really. Those are wonderful hyacinths you've got."

"Well, you want a bit of color sometimes, don't you?"

Carolus had dinner and picked up a novel which his cousin Fay had sent him as a Christmas present. The hours passed to ten

o'clock and, blissfully relaxed, he was about to go to bed when
the front door-bell was rung. He called to Mrs Stick that he would
open it, and did so to find Mullard there. He could see at once
that something was gravely amiss. Mullard spoke with a harsh,
almost contemptuous hostility. "I'm afraid," he said, "it was too
late to put a watch on 17, Marie Louise Avenue."

"Oh? Cara Myberg had gone?"

"No," replied Mullard icily. "Cara Myberg is dead." The two
men found themselves in chairs, Mullard still wearing his overcoat. There was a long silence.

"Poisoned, I take it?" said Carolus.

"Poisoned."

"Any chance of suicide?"

"I suppose so. In any other circumstances, suicide would be considered probable. But in view of her connection with the case . . ."

"Quite. Any reason to think Rathbone had been to the house?"

"Impossible to say. She had frequent callers. Her husband was
away. But the woman downstairs tells me that the day before
yesterday, in the evening, a man was ringing the Mybergs' bell for
some time without result. She herself, knowing that Mrs Myberg
was upstairs, let him in. A very respectable-looking, middle-aged
man, she says, in dark clothes. The house is divided up, as you
must have seen, but there are no front doors to each floor. She
heard this man knock, then open and shut a door. A few minutes
later she described him as 'bolting out of the house'."

"She could give no accurate description of the man, of course?"

"The usual thing. It could have been Rathbone, but it could
have been almost anyone of his age."

"It must have happened a few hours after I left her."

"Yes, Mr Deene. It seems to me you are rather more heavily
involved in this thing than you imagine. I don't know why you
took it upon yourself to go and see this woman. If you thought
she had any information, it was your duty to inform us. As it is,
you may be the last person to have seen her alive."

"Or the last but one," said Carolus reflectively.

18

CARA MYBERG had died of an overdose of luminal, a phenobarbital, but whether this was self-administered or not could not be decided at the inquest.

Carolus, abandoning his hope of a period of relaxation, once again put himself into the position of Rathbone in the hope of discovering his whereabouts. He imagined that the man, after hearing of the arrest of Oscar Gordon and realizing that it was almost certainly in mistake for himself, would feel very much more watched and observed than in reality he was. He saw him in London, not daring to register at a hotel, not daring to walk about the streets—though either might be safe enough—reaching despair and the agonies of fatigue.

Where would he, where could he go? Last time he had sought for a refuge, he had gone back to a place he had known in the past, the Lascelles Private Hotel. Was it too much to hope that now, half-crazy with fear, miserably tired, he might do the same? If so, it would not be to Lewisham, the scene of his unhappy boyhood, which he probably had not visited for years, and it could not be to Bolderton. Hastings was unlikely for he would remember Miss Ramble, who would certainly happen to be sitting in her window. But—it was a long chance—he might seek a brief rest at Glose Cottage. He had the key, he knew that Carolus was no longer there. In his dazed mind it would seem at least a place in which to stretch himself out to sleep. To reach it would not mean taking any great chances. When he had lived there, he had a car and would not be known to the railway staff. He could walk over from Tunney's Halt in twenty minutes and at least find a temporary peace.

But Carolus had a better reason for going back to Bluefield. There had come back to him something Mr Toffins had said about rubbish being tipped down a disused mine-shaft, and he had decided to know a little more about this. What an incomparable way of getting rid of . . . anything! If it served a large area, there would be tons of rubble and ash, of refuse of every kind tilted on top of whatever had been dropped. It would become virtually irrecoverable. A corpse, for instance—it would take a major mining operation and weeks of work and then the results would be dubious.

He drove down to Bluefield next afternoon, and at opening time received a rather cold greeting from Mr Lofting behind the bar of the Stag. Carolus compared him unfavorably with the landlord of the Porthaziel Hotel, who was a sound professional licensee and knew how a conversation should go between himself and a customer. Mr Lofting just now was busy with a youngish man wearing one of those silly little caps which looked as though it had been made for H. G. Wells to wear for cycling as a young man. Under it was an uncouth moustache.

"I thought as soon as you came in," said Lofting to this customer, "that's an Old Ravenstonedalean tie. I see you were in the NBLI, too." He had scarcely a glance for Carolus, so enraptured was he with his other visitor's insignia.

"Heard nothing more of the Rathbones, I suppose?" asked Carolus firmly.

"Not a thing," said Lofting briefly before turning back to his new acquaintance. "You must have been in Bangalore in '44, then? I thought I knew your face. Decent crowd at HQ, weren't they?"

Soon Mrs Luggett waddled in, and Carolus could buy her a "nice drop of stout" she said, because she didn't fancy draught beer in this weather. "You soon gave up living out there," she wheezed. "I thought you would. And just after I'd got the place a bit decent."

"Still, I expect you have plenty to do elsewhere," said Carolus.

"Well, I have and I haven't, as you might say. I don't mind giving any place a dust-over when it comes to that. I never take any notice of what's said."

"What is said?"

"Well, about Rathbones and that. Mind you, I never cared for that place, even if she wasn't buried under the floorboards. It had a nasty sort of smell with it, hadn't it?" She breathed stertorously before she finished her stout. "That's better!" she announced.

"What about a short?" asked Carolus.

"I don't mind a *rum*," said Mrs Luggett, making a special concession in favor of this spirit, as though whisky or gin would be highly unpleasant to her. "This cold weather seems to get into your bones, doesn't it?"

It would have a long way to go with Mrs Luggett, Carolus thought, but just then Mr Toffins came in and joined them. "You back, are you?" he said jovially. "Still asking about Rathbones? Last time you were here, it made me laugh to hear you go on about them. From all accounts it wasn't his wife that was here with him at all, then?"

"I don't take any notice of that," said Mrs Luggett equably. "Wife or no wife, I don't believe he done for her."

"No, but it's funny to think of him living with another woman and her buried where they lived before, or all that was left of her, according to what the papers say."

"Mr Toffins," put in Carolus, "when I was here before, you mentioned something about a disused mine-shaft being used for refuse?"

"That's right. Out at Grayfield, it is. They all come there to tilt their rubbish from Canterbury, Folkestone, everywhere."

"A good many lorries tilt there every day?"

"Scores of them. And it never will fill up. The mine hadn't been worked for I don't know how many years. They say there's no bottom to it, but that's just a tale. Anyhow, all that refuse goes right down out of sight and it's been going on for years now."

"Is the place enclosed?"

"Now it is. Barbed wire and a night watchman and everything. But that's only recently. A matter of a week or two before Christmas a horse and cart went to tilt when there was no one there and slipped back, it seems. The horse lost its foothold and down it went. Luckily the carter was standing clear or he'd have gone to perdition. So since then they've fenced it off and put a watchman on it, because you never know what might have gone down."

"You don't," agreed Carolus.

"I often laugh when I think that you could drop this whole village down there and no one the wiser."

"And not much loss, if you ask me," said Mrs Luggett, chuckling to make her chins crease and swell.

"Do you ever pass Glose Cottage now?" Carolus asked her.

"Of course I do. Every time I go home. My place is beyond there towards Tunney's Halt. I told you that."

"You should see her on her old bike!" said Mr Toffins. "You'd split your sides laughing. She doesn't half skip along though."

"You don't need to be shrivelled up to nothing to ride a bicycle," said Mrs Luggett.

"I suppose you never see anyone near Glose Cottage now?" Carolus pressed.

"Not since you left, I haven't."

"You'd notice it if anyone was there?"

"I should see the smoke and that, I suppose. I shall have to take a look since you're so interested."

"Thank you," said Carolus, and went up to the bar again. He felt like apologizing to Mr Lofting for his spotted and unsignificant tie, his lack of a blazer badge, his general failure to belong to the associations, clubs, societies and regiments which would have endeared him to the innkeeper. But he feared wartime reminiscences and old school fellowship too much to admit to Stonyhurst, Balliol and the Commandos, his modest record.

"This gentleman thinks he remembers meeting you in Tobruk, old man."

Carolus shook his head.

"What mob were you with during the war?"

"Ministry of Information," said Carolus, and ended a beautiful friendship. It was doubtful, in fact, whether Mr Lofting would let Carolus a room for the night, and he handed the matter to his wife as if to say that accommodation for such as this was beneath his notice. But next evening, as Carolus sat in the bar, Mrs Luggett waddled in and, flopping breathlessly into the seat beside him, gave him the news he had scarcely dared to expect.

"There's someone in there," she gasped. "Unless it's her walking shadow, poor thing, come back as they say they do to the place they knew last. Mind you, there's no smoke out of the chimney or anything. Oh, dear, that last pull up the hill will be the death of me. I feel as though I shall never get my breath again. Well, yes, I *will* have a nice drop of stout and see if that does any good, otherwise I'm sure I shall be done for."

When Carolus brought her stout, she lowered its Level in her glass by several inches. "That's better!" she sighed.

"You were telling me about Glose Cottage."

"Yes. This afternoon it was. After you asking about it, I had a good look as I came by this evening. I didn't stop or anything but peeped sideways, as you might say, not to be noticeable if there were people watching. Anyone my size can't go twisting and spinning this way and that like a teetotum. Still what I saw, I saw, and there's an end of it."

"What was it?" asked Carolus obligingly.

"Well, it was someone, I can't say more than that. Someone moving about. I didn't dare look too hard, but I'm not making any mistake. It wasn't just reflection on the window. I rode on pretty smartly as soon as I'd seen it, you may be sure of that. It was enough to give anyone the shudders to think of someone in that place right out there. But tonight when I came by I took a good look. I thought there might be a light burning. At first I was almost sure there wasn't. It looked dark as the grave. Well, thanks, I don't mind a drop of short when I remember what I've seen. It'll help to pull me together. I thought at first I should never be the same again."

Mrs Luggett wasted no time over her rum when she got it. It went down in a trice and there was deep if breathless appreciation in her "That's better!"

"Yes, it quite upset me what I saw," she said, returning to Glose Cottage. "Because it didn't seem like anything at first and only after I'd had a good look could I make it out. There was no light burning. Oh, no! Whoever it is in there's too artful for that. But after a minute I saw a sort of red glow. I thought to myself, so that's what they're up to. Waiting till after dark when no one can see the smoke coming out of the chimney, then lighting a fire. If that's not artful, I don't know what is."

Carolus went to the telephone, and after a time succeeded in speaking to Mullard at his home in Sidcup.

"I'm not giving you any definite information this time," he said, "and I won't be held responsible for anything that may come from my suggestion. But I think that if you come down to Blue-field very early tomorrow morning you will find Rathbone in the cottage he used to occupy."

Mullard was characteristically indignant. He hadn't had a decent night's sleep for days, he said, now *this*. How reliable was the information?

"It's not information at all," said Carolus. "It's just a friendly suggestion. It may lead to nothing whatever."

Mullard's indignation grew. He couldn't think why he had ever listened to Carolus. Here was this nonsense about Bluefield which, Carolus knew very well, he could not conscientiously ignore, yet which might lead to another wild-goose chase.

"Yes. It might," said Carolus mercilessly.

Was Mullard to get others out in the small hours and perhaps look a fool for doing so? This was the sort of thing Mullard most disliked about amateurs. Carolus kept maddeningly cool.

"I see your difficulty," he said. "But I've no intention of solving it for you. I simply tell you I have reason to think Rathbone may be there. I'm not particularly interested one way or the other. Catching criminals is not my job. I'm a dabbler and a theorist, not a policeman. But if you do come down, please come to breakfast with me at the Stag and, if it interests you, I'll tell you what I think about the whole thing."

"That," said Mullard with bitter sarcasm, "will be most enlightening, I'm sure. I suppose you know what has happened to the other women in this case? The Hastings one and the Bluefield one?"

"Oh, yes," said Carolus, "I know that. Also the Montgolfier Street one, the Marie Louise Avenue one, the Lascelles Private Hotel one, Anne Rathbone's sister and Anne Rathbone herself."

"You are omniscient. If I find Rathbone at Glose Cottage, I will accept your invitation to breakfast," said Mullard; "and we will hear this remarkable piece of romantic fiction."

Carolus was smiling as he put down the receiver and took it up again to ask for a Newminster number.

"This is the Headmaster's House of the Queen's School, Newminster," came the answer in a churchyard voice.

"Hullo, Headmaster," said Carolus gaily. "This is Deene. I wondered whether you would like to hear the end of this affair?"

"You have completed your investigations? You have worked out your theory?"

"One that satisfies me, anyway."

"Ah! And you intend to elucidate it for the benefit of those concerned?"

"I don't know who will benefit. I'm going to give the investigating CID man my explanation. No one else will be there unless you like to come."

"Where and at what hour?"

"Here in the Stag at Bluefield. Perhaps you would breakfast with me tomorrow?"

"But how, my dear Deene, do you suggest I should make the journey? You with your large automobile speak lightly of such jaunts. I have no means of transport."

"Surely . . ."

"Unless a certain Mrs Carruthers, the parent of that rather unpromising boy in the Lower Third, can be prevailed upon to run me down. She has frequently hinted that her car is at my disposal."

"Do that," said Carolus, "and I'll drive you back. What about Mrs Chalk? It was she who put me on to this case."

An almost passionate tone came into the headmaster's voice: "Mrs Chalk has only recently gone to stay with some relatives of her own in the salubrious town of Clacton-on-Sea. As a matter of fact, I went so far as to hint, lightly and tactfully of course, that she had perhaps misgauged our modest invitation. I think it would be most unwise, *most* unwise, to interrupt her visit."

"Just as you think," said Carolus. "I'll expect you about nine."

He went to make the difficult approach to Mr Lofting. He had to ask for a breakfast party from the innkeeper who now thought him of lesser breeds without the Law. He explained his difficulty.

"I don't know whether the wife will do it," said Mr Lofting sulkily. "Who did you say they were?"

"Mullard is a CID man," said Carolus hopefully. "Old Hendon Police Collegiate, if that's the right term." This made little impression. "The other is my boss. Headmaster of the Queen's School, Newminster."

"Is he, by Jove?"

"Yes. An Old Newbiggin-on-Lunean, I believe."

"That's different."

"London University," pressed Carolus. "Rowed, I seem to remember, for Lechlade-on-Thames Second Eight."

"War Service?" asked Mr Lofting.

"Home Guard!" cried Carolus triumphantly.

"I dare say we can manage it. Nine o'clock, you say? Yes. I'll speak to the wife."

Carolus slept soundly, quite undisturbed by the thought of the ugly little scene which he anticipated at Glose Cottage very early in the morning; but at barely half-past eight, when he came down to the small sitting-room behind the bar, he found Mullard awaiting him.

"Yes, we got him all right. I felt almost sorry for the poor wretch. He'd been lying up there eating what was left of the tinned stuff in the house and sleeping on a damp bed. He hadn't shaved for days and looked a pitiful specimen altogether. But then, I believe most of these wife-murderers do."

When Mr Gorringer arrived and he and Mullard had been introduced, they all three ate with a hearty appetite the ample breakfast Mrs Lofting provided. When the table was clear, the headmaster turned eagerly to Carolus. "We are all ears," he said, and for his own part it was nearly true.

"I scarcely know where to begin," Carolus reflected.

"Better begin with Anne Rathbone," suggested Mullard.

"Yes, tell us first, my dear Deene, how Rathbone killed his wife."

"But he didn't," said Carolus gently.

"I beg your pardon . . ." began Mr Gorringer.

"Rathbone didn't kill his wife. On the contrary he used every means, some of them quite extraordinary, to keep her alive."

19

When Mr Gorringer had recovered from this he spoke peremptorily: "Come then, Deene; let us have the whole story."

"I'll try," said Carolus; "but I dare say you'll find it all very long-winded and unconvincing. However . . . several conscientious Shakespearean critics—the term in itself's a paradox, by the way; who the hell is going to presume to criticize Shakespeare?—several of them have pointed out that each of the tragedies is the story of man being ruined by some particular fault which grew in him like a cancer. In Lear, it was vanity; in Macbeth, ambition; in Othello, jealousy; in Hamlet, procrastination. It's wildly to over-simplify, of course, but in our little story here it works out nicely. Rathbone was lazy, bone-lazy; I might almost say passionately lazy when I think of the very interesting account which Mullard gave me of his boyhood and when I recall the fire in his eyes when he said 'I have always hated work'. It was the key to his whole character. He was not at first an inhuman creature. He was a lazy young man whose interest could only vaguely be aroused by amateur theatricals. But that vice of his grew. I dare say he had some affection for Anne Bright when he married her. I felt he was speaking the truth when he said so, and good sensible Mrs Richards confirmed it. But I think the joy of marriage to him was that with his wife's comfortable income *he need never do another stroke of work in his life*. It simply did not occur to him, as it does not occur to others in his situation, that he might outlive his wife. She was some years younger than he was and he had never been a fit man. Yet that is exactly what happened. Anne became seriously ill with pernicious anaemia and, before the doctor could discover what was the basic cause of this, quite suddenly she died.

"Not long before, her sister Charlotte who was, in the words of the period, 'no better than she should be', had been down to see Anne, and Rathbone had her address. With the horror of work hanging over him—for Anne's income would die with her—he set himself to carry out a scheme which he had already in mind, perhaps for which the co-operation of Charlotte was necessary. This scheme was simplicity itself. It consisted in Rathbone's continuing to enjoy Anne's income after her death, with Charlotte as a stand-in for Anne.

"Anne's signature presented no difficulty. As I knew from Mrs Chalk, her handwriting was almost childish, and it would not be difficult for either or both of them to learn it. There were no inquisitive relatives, since the only interested parties, members of the Chalk family, were safely in Brazil. The trouble with the scheme was twofold—the disposal of Anne's body and the fact that, although the sisters were alike in features and voice, Charlotte was considerably plumper and healthier in appearance than the anaemic Anne. But they decided to chance that.

"These two people were drawn together, I think, by the bond of laziness, for prostitution itself is largely a form of that. Without being too cynical, that day-to-day existence is often the result of a lack of determination or set purpose. Both saw the advantages, an easy life on Anne's income. They must have talked it over at Coleshill Lodge, while Anne lay dead upstairs, and worked out their scheme. Charlotte never returned to the girl she lived with.

"Exactly how the body was disposed of, I do not intend to imagine, and I dare say you will be pleased if we do not dwell on this. But whatever means was adopted, fire or acid or whatnot, it left the head. There was really only one thing to be done with this and Rathbone did it. He buried it deeply under what was then a rubbish heap. That it was Rathbone's own scheme initially was shown by his dismissal of Mrs Richards on the morning after Anne's death. He must have thought about it for some time, for, instead of calling in the doctor when Anne was dying or dead, he left her that night, dismissed Mrs Richards when she arrived in the morning, and immediately summoned Charlotte. He had already dismissed the nurse, perhaps in anticipation. Then, since the doctor was not due till his weekly visit in the space of a day or two, Rathbone could put Charlotte in his car after dark and drive away with the stated intention of taking his wife to healthier surroundings.

"These they found in Hastings and, with some parade of arriving with an invalid wife, Rathbone moved into 47, Balaclava Grove. 'When they arrived here, Mrs Rathbone was so ill that she had to be carried into the house,' said Miss Ramble. There was only one way of avoiding a doctor and they took it. They let it be known that they were Christian Scientists and believed in self-cure. This was all right till the inquisitive Miss Ramble asked them about their religion and they knew so little that they had to refer her to a Christian Science reading-room. Charlotte remained immured for 'many weeks' before she could appear in the 'excellent health' she had always, in reality, had.

"When she did emerge, Charlotte only too soon revealed the cloven hoof and sang the unforgettably 'vulgar' song at the piano which so shocked Miss Ramble. She went on an occasional blind at the Star and Mitre. She was 'most sociable' and affable— a person very unlike the wilting Anne. Still, there was likeness enough to deceive Mumford's somewhat myopic clerk Potter, who had not seen Mrs Rathbone for years and concluded only that she had put on weight. After they had been at Hastings for about a year, they received what at first seemed a nasty shock. A policeman called and asked 'Mrs Rathbone' to come and identify her sister's body which had been found in Montgolfier Street. Fortunately for them, they kept their heads and said nothing till the policeman had gone.

"What had happened, of course, was that in Charlotte's hurried leaving of her friend, or rather in her failure to return to her after what was to have been a brief visit to her dying sister, she had left with the girl the only documents she had. When this girl who called herself Lucille French was found dead, the police searched her possessions and discovered the letter which Mumford had written to Charlotte about her thousand-pound legacy. It was the only clue to poor Frenchy's identity. Heaven knows who she was or where she came from, but 'Mrs Rathbone' identified her as Charlotte Bright and as such she was cremated.

"From one point of view this simplified the situation. Charlotte was now officially dead and cremated, and Rathbone remained married to a marvellously recovered 'Anne', a credit to the ozone of Hastings. This might have continued for years, and the two might have deceived even the watchful Mrs Chalk, when she returned from Brazil, since she and Charlotte had scarcely met. But a new cloud arose on Rathbone's horizon. The ease and rest which he had sought were soon dispersed again, this time more dangerously. When all seemed to go smoothly and the income came in pleasant quarterly instalments, and nobody dreamed that there was anything odd about Mr and Mrs Rathbone of Balaclava Grove, and Coleshill Lodge was reoccupied and all seemed well, the most unexpected and ironic thing had to happen—Charlotte fell in love."

"Come now, Deene," put in Mr Gorringer. "You have told us that she was nothing better than a common prostitute."

"Perhaps you haven't made much close study of the species," said Carolus. "I can assure you there was nothing unprecedented about this event. The man she fell for was a commercial traveller and very soon the Rathbones' neighbors on both sides, who both of them chanced to be at the window on all strategic occasions, were aware of what was going on."

"What was the commercial traveller's name?" asked Mullard.

"Myberg."

"Halt!" cried Mr Gorringer. "A word of explanation here! Are you telling us, my good Deene, that Charlotte Bright, the sister of the deceased Anne Rathbone, the woman known as Cara, the friend of the dead girl called Lucille French, the pretended wife of Rathbone at Hastings, afterwards became none other than that unfortunate Mrs Myberg found dead from an overdose of luminal?"

"That is what I'm telling you. Why?"

"Incredible!" said Mr Gorringer. "So the 'second Mrs Rathbone' was not murdered as the people of Hastings suspected?"

"Suspicions of murder in Hastings at that time, if they existed, were wholly misplaced. Charlotte left Rathbone to live with Myberg, even, for all I know, to marry him."

"This grows more murky and curious than I dreamed," said Mr Gorringer with a solemn shake of his head.

"How do you know that Cara Myberg was Charlotte Bright?" asked Mullard sharply.

"It was fairly obvious from the first. Rathbone would never have dared put his scheme into action unless he had Anne's sister to help him, and there was sufficient likeness between them to deceive the solicitors who acted for their father. Moreover, who *else* could have driven away from Bolderton with him? Who else would have identified Frenchy as Charlotte Bright? But I had better reasons than these. Mrs Myberg gave herself away hopelessly when I saw her. She was supposed to be 'Cara', a friend of 'Frenchy' who had died and been identified by her sister, when I knew that in fact that sister had died years before at Bolderton, so she was in an impossible position from the first. She was supposed only to have heard of Rathbone from her friend Frenchy, who was supposed to have met him once. Yet the first thing she said, when I asked her if she knew Rathbone, was 'yes'; then tried to cover it by adding that she knew him by name. If she had been a mere acquaintance of Charlotte, she was unlikely to know anything of Mrs Chalk, whom Charlotte herself had scarcely met; yet as soon as I mentioned Mrs Chalk, Mrs Myberg said: 'Oh, that bitch! What's she got to do with it? She scarcely knew Anne.' This was said in that feelingly intimate tone which could only be used of a personally known and disliked acquaintance. There were lots of other small indications during the interview I had with Mrs Myberg. 'That thousand pounds,' she said and knew that it came from the mother. But most of all there was the state of abject terror into which she was thrown when I told her, right at the end of the interview, what I wanted to know from Maurice Myberg, and what the police would want to know. 'Where he met you,' I said, quite casually, and left her in a condition of uncontrollable fear and perturbation. For they met at Hastings and from that she would very soon be identified as 'the second Mrs Rathbone' and from that as Charlotte Bright, who had helped to dispose of her sister's body perhaps, and had certainly been guilty of fraud over a number of years. There was no reasonable doubt about the identity of Mrs Myberg as Cara and as Charlotte Bright. It was all very clear up to that point."

With sepulchral rumblings Mr Gorringer cleared his throat. "It is but eleven o'clock," he said, "yet I feel that this exhausting analysis merits for Deene some refreshment, and I suggest that you and I, Inspector, should join him. What say you?"

There was a break of a few minutes while they were served and, as Mr Gorringer put it, regaled themselves. "A point which leaves me at a loss," complained the headmaster presently, "is that recent visit by the Rathbones to the solicitors when the life interest had been disposed of."

"As to the why of that I hope to explain in a moment. The how of it was simple enough. Though Charlotte or Cara had left Rathbone and was living with Myberg, she was called in for the sake of one last deception, for which she doubtless received a handsome reward, if not a half-share of the total obtained— fraudulently, of course, since Anne was dead long before—from the finance company which had taken over the life income. That accounts for an apparently genuine 'Mrs Rathbone' being at Mumford's offices when it seemed impossible. Incidentally it would be further proof, if that were needed, that 'Cara' and not 'Frenchy', who was dead by then, had started life as Charlotte Bright.

"An interesting fact arose from Miss Ramble's reminiscences. So soon after 'the second Mrs Rathbone' had left Rathbone at Hastings did he himself leave the town that it caused considerable question and comment. Let me quote Miss Ramble when I asked her if Rathbone left soon after his wife. 'Almost immediately,' she said, after telling me of the suggestion that he had done away with his wife. The truth was that the quarter was nearly up and another cheque would be due. Rathbone had to find a new wife as swiftly as possible and take her to a part of the country where he was not known. There was no going back for him now. He would be charged with the murder of Anne almost certainly, and *quite* certainly he would face a long term of imprisonment for fraud. His only chance, as he saw it, was to find a substitute for Charlotte, who at least could be relied on not to talk; she was herself too deeply involved for that. So he moved his furniture to London hoping—and his hopes were justified—that his neighbors, though watchful, might not have the bare-faced curiosity to take the trouble to trace him through that.

"I had a fairly good idea of all this when I went down to Bolderton and saw Mrs Richards. It was the details she gave me of Rathbone's behavior at the time of his wife's illness which convinced me: how he dismissed the nurse and how, so suddenly and seeming 'very upset', one morning he dismissed Mrs Richards herself, saying he was going to take his wife to live by the sea; he would not even let Mrs Richards clear up, but gave her three weeks' money to go at once; he himself remained in the house some days after she had left.

"I had been lucky in this case in dealing with people who have excellent memories. Dr Whistley, for example, who had attended Anne Rathbone at Bolderton, was most explicit. And my friend 'Old Maree' and *her* friend Elizabeth were very helpful.

It was 'Old Maree' who made me realize that 'Cara' was Charlotte and 'Frenchy' an unknown girl, and not vice versa. It was through 'Old Maree' that I was able to trace Cara. Her description of Cara tallied nicely with Miss Ramble's description of the 'second Mrs Rathbone'. I felt surer at every moment. 'Old Maree' remembered, too, how very suddenly Cara disappeared, as she did when Rathbone put his proposition to her. Then Mr Villiers, formerly Schmidt, was most informative. In his information about Rathbone as an employee, as a member of the Amateur Dramatic Society and as a lover to the uninteresting daughter of the firm's rich chartered accountant, he aided me considerably. It was also through him that, partly by chance, I picked up the later trail of Rathbone. But we shall come to that. At the moment I want to clear up all the odds and ends of my theory—for I do not regard it as more—up to the point when Charlotte or 'Cara' had left Rathbone at Hastings, and within a few days he himself disappeared leaving a cloud of suspicion behind him."

"You've done that," said Mullard, "and, as long as you are content to call it theory, I see no harm in it. It won't prevent us charging Rathbone with the murder of his wife."

"No? You think he murdered Anne?"

"I *ask* you!" said Mullard. "We find the woman's skull buried three feet deep under concrete six years after she disappears and you ask me whether I *think* Rathbone murdered her. Who else could have?"

"I don't know. I don't believe in her murder but, if it happened, it was not done by Rathbone. Of that I am quite certain."

"Although he lived alone with her? Dismissed the nurse and the daily help? Disappeared suddenly and recently, after another sudden vanishing by another wife? Has been dodging us all over the place? Of course he killed her. What possible reason can you have for doubting it?"

"The entire, absolute lack of any kind of motive."

"There, Mr Deene, you must allow an experienced police officer to know a little bit more than you can possibly know.

Lack of motive! That's an academic illusion. Half the murders we investigate have no motive that would seem a motive to anyone but the murderer. These psychopathic cases and sex crimes aren't in the category of cause and motive at all. What motive had Jack the Ripper, do you suppose?"

"In his own mind, a very adequate one I am sure. But we're not dealing here with a psychopath or a sexual maniac. Rathbone is as sane as you or I."

"You believe that Anne died naturally?"

"I am sure of it. Her death was the very last thing Rathbone wanted. All his crimes have been committed in trying to put right that blow of fate."

Mr Gorringer indicated by another stormy rumble that he was about to join in the conversation. "Interesting as it is to a layman like myself to hear these polemics from such experts as you," he enunciated, "I feel that I should give the opinion of a plain man. It seems to me that the truth in the matter of the unfortunate Anne Rathbone will only be apparent when we learn the fate of her successors. Inspector Mullard opines that Rathbone was a psychopathic case, a criminal motivated by the dim and horrible promptings of some sexual aberration. Deene, on the other hand, claims that he was nothing of the sort. Let us then hear the sequel. Let us know the truth about the other sudden deaths in this case. We know that Anne Bright's father opposed her marriage to Rathbone and died suddenly. We know that the woman known as 'Frenchy' was found dead in a room in the notorious precincts of Montgolfier Street. We know that Mrs Myberg has recently died as the result of an overdose of luminal. Let us hear about these from Deene. Above all let us know what befell the woman known as 'the third Mrs Rathbone'."

Carolus looked puzzled. "But there was no 'third Mrs Rathbone'," he said. "Surely that must have been obvious to you?"

"Ah," said Mr Gorringer, "some facetious word-play of yours, Deene. Come now. Tell us all."

20

"As to the other deaths you mention," went on Carolus, "I don't think we need waste much time on them. It would be an insult to the medical profession to suppose that there was anything questionable about the death of Herbert Bright, and I have not even bothered to see the doctor who signed his death certificate. Cases of food poisoning above all are most carefully scrutinized. If the faintest suspicion had existed, if the doctor who attended the old gentleman had not known exactly what caused his death, there would have been an autopsy.

"Much the same is true of 'Frenchy'. The women who lived in that house talked glibly about the doctor giving the 'usual' certificate, but that is part of their characteristic self-pity. There is nothing extraordinary about the death in such circumstances of a prostitute, and it is absurd to try to connect Rathbone with it. I doubt if he knew of 'Frenchy's' existence, unless Charlotte casually mentioned it to him.

"But the case of Mrs Myberg is somewhat different, and in a certain way I feel myself to blame, for it was I who indicated to her, beyond any possible doubt, that I knew of her part in this affair. I think perhaps, as I study my own motives now, that I wanted to warn her. My interest in crime begins and ends with murder; I have no wish to be responsible for the punishment of offenders against any law but the sixth commandment. Cara Myberg had assisted in an ingenious fraud and in the illegal destruction of a corpse, but she had killed no one. I am not arguing the ethics of the thing, merely stating the limitations of my interest.

"However, the wretched woman did not realize that and believed that she would shortly be convicted of several serious crimes including, perhaps, complicity in the murder of Anne, for she may have foreseen Mullard's attitude. No doubt further investigation will reveal more, but in the meantime I am convinced that she committed suicide. The inquest has been adjourned, I believe, and there may be more evidence later. I admit that Rathbone may have been to her house shortly after her death; that again seems to me irrelevant though I am not dogmatic about it. We shall come to Rathbone's recent behavior in a few minutes.

"We left him driving away from Hastings in search of a secluded home and someone who would assist him in keeping up the deception which could not now be dropped. Perhaps he knew already of that grim and lightly populated area which lies in the sprawling rectangle formed by the roads between Canterbury, Dover, Folkestone and Ashford. At any rate, he found Bluefield, and in Glose Cottage just the dwelling he wanted. Soon after I began to make inquiries about the Rathbones and their life at Bluefield, I noticed a curious phenomenon: most local people knew the Rathbones by sight, most described them singly, *but never the two together*.

"Drubbing, for instance, the first person I met, knew Rathbone, who had been in his office. Of Mrs Rathbone he said he did not know her and had only seen her driving the car. Then Wallbright the postmaster: '*He* came in now and again for cigarettes or stamps but I can't remember *her* ever being in the shop.'

Then the woman who supplied teas in Bluefield village: 'I used to see her in church. She used to sit right at the back and nip out almost before it was over. He was a bit more sociable. He *has* been known to pop into the Stag. But not her. She never did any shopping in the village.' Lofting the publican: 'The man came in here occasionally.' When asked if Mrs Rathbone accompanied him: 'Good Lord, no! She was supposed to be strictly TT.' The postman, Fred Spender: 'I've seen her. Not to say often, but more than anyone else, I dare say. Didn't talk much. Just "thank you" when I handed her the letters. He was just the opposite. Gloomy-looking. But he would now and again exchange a few words.' The Rector knew Rathbone but 'never had a chance' to speak to his wife, though he saw her in church. Dr Chatto was never called to the house, Rathbone only consulting him at the surgery.

"Mr Toffins was perhaps the most revealing about this. 'It would have made you laugh. To have seen *one or the other*, I mean.' Then he went on to describe them individually. No one seemed ever to have seen them together and that for a very simple reason. They were not two people but one."

Mr Gorringer gave his throaty and rather patronizing chuckle. "So we are to abandon all sense of reality," he said with a glance at Mullard to see if he gave support, "and enter the realms of sheer fantasy. We are Alice passing through the looking-glass. How in the world do you suppose such a deception could be practised successfully for a day, let alone for three years?"

"It was just those three years, that passage of time, which made it feasible. The *alter ego* became a familiar figure. Rathbone, you see, was tired of trusting his freedom, well-being and, most important, his *ease*, to a woman who might do such a thing as Charlotte had done and decide to leave him. Why, after all, was it necessary? He had long ago learned Anne's signature and the only thing that could stop the quarterly payments was the announcement of Anne's death. All he needed was to appear to be a married man. He had a good deal in his favor. He had a certain skill in make-up, enough, anyway to avoid complicated effects or ones which would take a long time to assume. He had also a mobile face which lent itself to the thing. 'Effeminate', the Rector of Bluefield called him, and explained it by saying that there was 'a sort of softness or weakness' in Rathbone's face.

"It would be interesting to know how he obtained the wardrobe. 'Old-fashioned' it was described in Bluefield, and that seems to have been no exaggeration. The wig was a natural one for a middle-aged woman, and if you, Inspector, think it necessary, I can let you have several hairs from it that I found in Glose Cottage. As for teeth, he had a simple but ingenious idea. He wore his dentures as Mrs Rathbone and left them out as Rathbone. As he had a perpetual smile as Mrs Rathbone, the teeth were noticeable, but his own gaps, when Rathbone, were noticed, too, particularly by the Rector, who remarked on them to me. That must have changed the two faces considerably.

"The beauty of this disguise, if we must call it that, was that it was a quick-change affair. The wig, the ear-rings, the dentures, the thick spectacles, a dab or two of powder and the clothes—Rathbone could become Mrs Rathbone, as he did once while Toffins was unloading his coal. Only one thing could give him away— his hands. He was forced to keep these in beautiful condition to be ready for their appearance as Mrs Rathbone's, and this did not go well with his slipshod appearance and indolent character. Dr Chatto noticed them. 'Extraordinary thing,' he said, 'the man neglected his teeth and looked generally pretty seedy, but he had small well-kept hands.'

"But with his appearance he was wise enough to change his manner. The sad-looking, shifty man, who never smiled but usually greeted people in a dismal sort of way, became the cheery-looking, perpetually smiling but almost monosyllabic woman. 'Mrs Rathbone' does not seem to go on record in Bluefield as having said more than 'thank you' once or twice, and even that may be faulty memory on the hearer's part. If someone smiles and nods and makes some sound, it is probable that it would be recollected afterwards as 'saying thank you'. But that's as may be.

The feminine part of the personality had no cause to say more. She never left her house except in the car. It was easy for Rathbone to open the door as himself on any occasion which might lead to difficulties, like the Rector's ill-fated call.

"Once created, the 'third Mrs Rathbone' had considerable advantages over her predecessors. She cost nothing to maintain and she could not suddenly want to go away. She did not answer back or want to go to the local like the second, or cost a lot in doctor's bills like the first. All Rathbone had to do from morning to night and from year's end to year's end was to receive the quarterly cheque, do a little housework—and it *was* a little as I discovered when I moved in—and occasionally amuse himself with the 'amateur theatricals' of becoming Mrs Rathbone. The life suited him admirably and looked like continuing indefinitely.

"But 'man is born to trouble, as the sparks fly upward', and Rathbone never seemed fated to enjoy the bliss of idleness for long. Just as he had worked out this pleasant routine of lotus-eating, he received a letter which at once shattered the dream. Mrs Chalk was leaving Brazil for England and looked forward to seeing her cousin Anne. She was the *one* person in the world who could neither be hoodwinked nor bribed, since it was her children who were losing by the scheme—had already, in fact, been losing for six years.

"Rathbone was desperate. He formed a foolish plan of cashing in as best he could on the life income and going abroad in the hope that he would not be extradited. For this he needed Cara Myberg and, as we have seen, she accompanied him to Mumford's office. But even then he could not make up his mind. Perhaps this was a very brief visit by Mrs Chalk, and she would not have time to search for Anne if he told her she had left him? After all, he could flee after her visit if he seemed to be threatened—there would be plenty of time. So, like many indolent people, he dithered on till it was too late and Mrs Chalk was upon him.

"But in the meantime he eliminated 'the third Mrs Rathbone' by the simple process of burning her shoes, clothes and wig. But he forgot the ear-rings until the last moment, and Mrs Chalk actually interrupted him burying them in his favorite place—under the rubbish heap. Of all these, traces have since been found. I had the ashes of the grate expertly examined and they were found to contain burnt cloth, while among them were shoemaker's tacks. The fingerprint situation was an interesting one, since certain fingerprints left in grease or whatnot in a kitchen would endure for weeks and, of course, the only prints found were Rathbone's. Although he had attempted to clean all prints, I am convinced that, if such a person as 'the third Mrs Rathbone' had existed as a separate entity, some of her prints would have been there.

"Mrs Chalk noticed that he had shaved his moustache, as he had been forced to do for the sake of his quick changes of personality. He had arranged to sell his furniture by auction, giving Mrs Chalk the reason that Anne had left him, but after her visit, and her warning that she would not leave England till she had found her cousin, he panicked and disappeared. I don't know where he went while he grew his moustache, but not much later he turned up at the boarding-house in which he had lived more than fifteen years ago. He now became the jaunty Colonel Hood.

"It was partly by chance that I found him there. Villiers gave me the address of the place in which Rathbone had lived when he worked for Tonkins, and I went there in hope of picking up some information. I only waited to see Colonel Hood because I thought he might have known Rathbone in the old days. I had, as you know, already met Rathbone on his nocturnal visit to Glose Cottage to recover his forgotten cheque book and, when he saw me again, he realized that once more he would have to go. But I told him something which scared the wits out of him—that the police would soon make as thorough a search of the house and garden at Coleshill Lodge as they had done at Glose Cottage. I knew pretty well what effect this would have. I was convinced from his manner that something incriminating was concealed there, and I believed that he would try to recover it."

Mr Gorringer broke in. "Let us pause again," he suggested, "before you give us the last details. I have not wished to interrupt you, but for some time I have noticed that Inspector Mullard's glass is empty."

"By all means," said Carolus, and laid down his notes.

"I must admit," Mullard conceded, "that I begin to find your theory more tenable than it seemed."

"But you do not know our Deene!" chuckled Mr Gorringer. "He is keeping, I warrant, some surprise for the end. It is his way."

"No, Headmaster," said Carolus rather wearily. "You have had all the surprises—if they *were* surprises—which the case offers. The rest is just odds and ends of information."

"We shall see," said Mr Gorringer.

After a drink and a few deep pulls at one of his favorite cheroots, Carolus proceeded: "The present occupant of Coleshill Lodge was most helpful; in fact when he heard what I anticipated, he entered into the spirit of the thing and would like to have shared my vigil. This was rewarded, but in a way that surprised me. I never for a moment anticipated that Rathbone would assume one of his former disguises for his visit and the motive is still somewhat obscure. It must have cost him considerable trouble and expense, since he had destroyed the appurtenances of 'the third Mrs Rathbone'. Perhaps he feared recognition in that area in which he had lived so long, but it was scarcely likely that anyone would see and know him at one or two o'clock in the night. He was by this time in a state of such panic that he was capable of some quite crazy actions.

"It was, then, dressed as 'the third Mrs Rathbone', that he entered the garden and received the severest blow he had yet suffered, for he saw that over the spot where Anne's skull was buried a summer-house had been built. He fled and, as I fortunately realized in the morning, he went into yet deeper hiding, assuming his most intelligently considered disguise as yet. I reached St Andrew's Avenue just before he made his departure from the Lascelles Private Hotel and was able to follow him to Waterloo, from which he left for Cornwall. On the journey he ceased to be Colonel Hood and assumed a personality with which he could have remained secure in the art colonies of Cornwall for as long as his money lasted; but the wretched creature was put to flight again by the arrest of Oscar Gordon, which he rightly supposed was in mistake for his own arrest.

"Now he *was* in despair. The only refuge he could think of was at Cara Myberg's, since he had no reason to think she had yet been drawn into the net of investigation. (She had visited him several times at the Lascelles Private Hotel, by the way, doubtless to talk over their common danger.) When he found her dead, he lost his head altogether and, with the four horsemen of the Apocalypse on his heels, he dropped on to his old bed at Glose Cottage in which, he remembered, he had left some tinned food. It was there that you found him this morning. I imagine his arrest came almost as a relief to him."

"So that's your case?" said Mullard almost kindly.

"That's my case. There are some loose ends which you will be able very easily to tie up. For instance, on the night he visited Coleshill Lodge he came by car. Since he had not then a car of his own he must have either hired one or stolen one. That should be a confirming detail, but I don't think you'll need even that. Rathbone will tell you the whole story quite readily and probably plead guilty to fraud and his offences in the matter of Anne's body. But he won't plead guilty to a murder, because he has not committed one."

"No surprises!" Mr Gorringer almost shouted. "You said there would be no surprises, Deene, yet here we have the greatest surprise of all! You dangle before our eyes, as it were, already hanging on a gibbet, a mass-murderer, a monster in human shape, answerable for the fiendish crime of murdering certainly three and possibly as many as five persons in the most cold-blooded manner. Then you proceed to demonstrate with your inimitable gift of persuasion, if not always with the logic and reliable evidence we could wish, that no murder at all has taken place. Is not that a surprise to end all surprises, to use a popular phrase? Is not that *étonnant, épatant, extraordinaire?*"

"I shouldn't have thought so," said Carolus carelessly, as he lit another cheroot.